# HARRIET HALL AND THE MIRACLE CURE

## SONIA GARRETT

Paperback ISBN 978-1-7750106-4-7

Ebook ISBN 978-1-7750106-5-4

*For Jacquie*

# CONTENTS

# CHAPTER ONE
## EVACUATE
### THE ROYAL NAVAL COLLEGE, LONDON, ENGLAND—MAY 1940

Five fighter planes flew in formation over the manicured lawns of the Royal Naval College. Their engines shook the ground and rattled the wooden boards covering the windows.

"I bet I could touch one of their bombs if I climbed up here," Harriet Hall shouted.

Emily Esme Black, known as Bee, watched as her best friend lassoed her jump rope around the statue of the Duke of Wellington. Harriet smiled to herself when she spotted Bee glancing around nervously. The enormous granite buildings of the Royal Naval College seemed deserted. Somewhere, men were training for war, but the paths and porticos were empty.

"We'll get in trouble again if we're found climbing the statues," Bee said.

"Who's going to stop us?" Harriet asked. "The grown-ups are too busy dealing with Hitler. As long as we don't break anything and we're home by curfew, no one cares."

"I think I'm going to my aunt's place in the country," Bee said.

"You can't! You said we'd be together forever."

"Aren't you being evacuated? After the bomb landed in the

schoolyard, Mom said I have to leave. It was too close for comfort."

Harriet thrust her chin in the air. "I'm not leaving! No one can make me."

Harriet Hall pulled the rope tight and checked it would take her weight. She placed her feet on the marble pillar and climbed to the top.

"Come on, Bee," Harriet said. "Try it."

Harriet reached the top just as the next group of planes filled the sky. She stretched her arms above her head and formed Churchill's V for Victory with her index and middle fingers. Then, she held on with her knees and reenacted an aerial dogfight with the Luftwaffe bombed from the sky.

Harriet thought of her father, commanding an enormous battleship, blasting the German U-boats out of his way. He'd be home soon. Victorious. Or so they were told. She refused to believe the bombed schoolyard, crater-filled roads and collapsed houses told a different story—one of the losing side. In Harriet's mind, evacuees were rats escaping a fire. They were weak, scared and cowardly.

The sound of boots jolted Harriet out of her thoughts. Bee reacted like a startled squirrel. She ran across the lawn, up the stairs, and hid behind a pile of sandbags. Harriet tucked her body into Wellington's back.

"Company, halt! Attention!"

Twenty naval officers in starched white uniforms came to a stop.

"Miss Hall, kindly get down from our great leader's memorial and show some respect," Lieutenant Gordon said.

"My father gives the orders, not you," Harriet mumbled.

"What was that?"

"Nothing," Harriet said.

"Nothing, what?"

"Nothing, sir." Harriet replied through gritted teeth.

"Now, run along home. London is no place for a child. It'd

be better for us if your mother evacuated you," Lieutenant Gordon said.

"You can't make me! If the King can stay in Buckingham Palace, then I can stay in my home as well. And I'm not a child. I'm twelve years old."

"And there, gentlemen, is the generation we're fighting for."

Twenty men looked at Harriet and laughed.

"Company about face! March two, three, four."

Harriet climbed down from the statue and stomped over to join her friend.

"I'd better go," Bee said. "Mother will be so angry if I'm not home for dinner."

"Come on. We'll take the shortcut through the college."

"I'm not allowed. Mom says the dining room is for officers and they don't want anyone spoiling their peace."

Harriet threw her arms up in frustration. "Then we'd better tell Adolf Hitler not to drop bombs at teatime. Grown-ups will not worry about a couple of kids taking a shortcut to make sure they get home safely."

Harriet leaned on the enormous door to the Royal Naval College and opened it just enough for her body to squeeze through. She turned and saw Bee grinning quietly. Secretly, Harriet knew her friend enjoyed breaking the rules, as long as it wasn't her idea.

The two girls walked through the entrance, up the marble stairs and into the dining hall. Bee stood mesmerized under the painted ceiling. Harriet followed her gaze. Cherubs on clouds stared back at them.

"I'd forgotten how beautiful they are," Bee said.

"You know if you stare at them for too long, an actual angel will fall all the way from heaven to hell," Harriet said.

Bee spun around. "They will not! Harriet Hall, you're such a liar! Your nose will grow bigger than Pinocchio's," Bee said. "I hope the Luftwaffe doesn't drop their bombs here. Imagine this place turned to rubble."

"They wouldn't dare," Harriet said.

"But my mother says nothing is safe—schools, hospitals, people, even the College." Bee bit her lip and looked into Harriet's eyes. "Hitler will bomb everything until we surrender. That's why I'm being sent away."

"You can't. We made a plan to stick together, whatever happens."

Bee jumped when she heard footsteps. Harriet grabbed her hand, and they ran behind a screen into the kitchen. The noise of pots and pans, cutting and cooking made it impossible for Harriet to hear Bee's objections.

"What are you doing in here?" a cook shouted. "Get out, this is no place for you or your games."

"Run," Harriet shouted.

They dodged past the cook and bumped into a man carrying a tray of cutlery. Bee heard the angry shouts as the cutlery crashed to the floor. She pushed open a door and raced outside. The fresh air felt good. Bee looked over her shoulder to check no one had followed them. They were alone. No one had the time to chase kids. The girls stood and caught their breath. Harriet laughed when she saw her friend's pale face.

"You are such a worrywart, we're almost home," Harriet said. "I'll see you tomorrow."

"Maybe not."

Bee held out her arms. It looked as if her best friend was about to hug her. This was too weird. Normally, they'd just go their own way, and Harriet refused to believe her life would change because of one bomb crater in their school playground. Everyone had lost their gumption. Harriet dug her shoe into the tiny pebbles covering the courtyard.

"Don't be soft," Harriet said. "I'll see you tomorrow."

Bee looked at her friend. There was a moment when Harriet thought Bee was about to say something. Instead, Bee turned and ran across the gravel. Harriet drew a heart in the pebbles using the scuffed toe of her shoe. There were times she wanted a brave friend, but she kind of enjoyed being boss. Bee never wanted to take charge. Harriet drew the letters H and B in the heart. They'd be friends forever.

There was a damp, smoky feel in the air. Harriet walked to a wooden crate, sat and stared at the sky. She didn't want to go home, and she didn't want to think about Bee leaving London.

It would be hours before sunset, but Harriet thought she'd seen the twinkle of a star. She sifted through the wishes she could make. She could always ask for her mother's health to return but, night after night, those wishes went unheard. Hundreds, maybe thousands, would ask for the war to end, but Harriet liked war. Sure, she wanted her father at home, smoking his pipe by the fire, but with him away, scuffed shoes weren't a problem. Plus, she liked telling stories about her father commanding battleships. War excited her—the uniforms, airplanes, air raid drills. Adults even talked about closing schools. There'd be no one left to tell her what to do and when to do it. A shudder passed through her body. Of course, she wanted her mummy and daddy to survive, that went without saying. It was the teachers and school rules she would happily live without. Harriet stood up, stretched out her arms and spun in the empty courtyard.

A tiny meow caught her attention. It was so weak Harriet strained to hear it.

"Hello," Harriet said. "Hello, where are you?"

She followed the sound to the garbage cans. The stink was horrendous, old vegetable peelings, fish and putrid meat. The rest of England had food rations, but here, at the naval college, they seemed to throw stuff away. Harriet squeezed past the metal cans and found a cat so thin all its bones were showing. It had a gash across its face as if it had been in a fight. The cat looked from Harriet to the garbage bin, placed her paws on the huge container and tried to knock it over.

"Come with me," Harriet said.

She reached down and stroked its fur. The animal was soaking wet and mewing hopelessly.

"You poor thing," Harriet said.

Harriet wrapped the cat in her coat and gently cradled it in her arms as she walked the few yards home.

Two things struck Harriet as she pushed open her front door. The first were the suitcases in the hall. The second was her mother leaning against the sideboard, struggling for breath.

"Harriet, you're late," she wheezed. "Be a dear and switch all the lights out."

"But it'll be hours before it gets dark," Harriet said. "And why are our bags packed?"

"We're leaving first thing in the morning."

Harriet's stomach flipped, her eyes widened, and it felt as if someone had put a ton weight on her chest. Concrete was setting around Harriet's heart, and she wanted to scream to make sure it kept beating.

"No! We can't leave! I won't leave without Father!" Harriet cried.

"Please, Harriet, I don't have the energy to argue," Mrs. Hall said. "Mrs. Peters made you a sandwich. It's on the kitchen table. Take it to your room, once you've put whatever flea-bitten creature you have in your coat outside where it belongs. We both need a good night's sleep before we set off."

Harriet clung to the cat, stormed into the kitchen, took out a bottle of milk, and poured some into a saucer. Then she took the food, milk and stray bundle upstairs. She sat on the top step and listened.

Harriet was aware of her mother shuffling from room to room, doing the chore she'd asked Harriet to do. One by one, lights went out. Harriet refused to feel guilty. It wasn't her fault her mother was sick and London doctors couldn't get her better. Harriet pulled the cat close to her chest and heard a quiet purr. The house would soon be dark. Her mother would go to bed and leave her alone. Harriet walked slowly to her room, placed the furry bundle under her bedspread and reached for a flashlight. She made a cozy tent around them. The cat lapped the milk and eyed the sandwich. Harriet broke off a corner, fed it to her new pet and reached for the worn copy of *Little House on the Prairie*. Tomorrow, she'd pretend to be an American pioneer with Bee.

There was a knock on her door.

Harriet poked her head out from under the bedspread and held the cat under the covers.

"I can smell the stray, Harriet. I asked you to put it outside."

"But Mummy…"

Harriet reached under her blanket, pulled the cat into her arms and allowed its head to appear. The tiny pink nose, long whiskers and enormous eyes stared back at her. No one could force her to release something so small and loving. Harriet knew she could never leave it behind.

"No buts. We can't take it with us."

"Please, please Mummy. It'll be able to catch mice as soon as she's better. Daddy would let me keep her."

"Your father has found us somewhere safe to live until the war ends. He wrote to us both. Here's his letter to you. This explains things better than I can," Harriet's mother said. "Read it then turn off your flashlight before blackout begins."

Harriet took the parchment in her hand. Her name was written in the rough cursive script of her father's handwriting. She held the paper to her face. There was no smell of tobacco, no roughness of his evening stubble, no warmth of an embrace. Her eyes prickled. It was nearly a year since Harriet's father, Captain James Hall, had marched off at the head of his company and away to war.

She loosened her grip on the cat, unfolded the letter and read it repeatedly.

My darling Princess,

If you are reading this, your mother and I have found a safe passage for you both to get to Canada. You will be happy there. You have three cousins to play with. The air is clean. Your mother will feel better, and you'll be far away from this nasty business with Mr. Hitler. There are forests, lakes and mountains to explore. Adventures abound, and I'll know you are safe.

I'll join you as soon as I can.

Until then, bon voyage, my beautiful angel.

Love from

Daddy

"Canada?" Harriet whispered as she stroked the cat in her lap. "We're going to Canada?"

## CHAPTER TWO
## BOYS!
### LOUGHLIN MILLS, BRITISH COLUMBIA, CANADA—JULY 1940

Harriet held a jump rope in her hands. She wanted to hear what the boys were saying, while pretending she wasn't interested. Her cousin, Robert Davis, whispered to his younger brothers, Billy and Mickey. They were all stuck in the yard again. For an entire week she'd been told, "Run along and play with your cousins, but don't leave the yard." Harriet was living through the worst summer of her life. When she'd arrived, they'd celebrated with a picnic down by the lake while Harriet's mother rested to regain her strength after the long journey. Since then, Harriet had been stuck in this house and yard. Robert, only two years older than her, got to work at the family bakery every morning, but she went nowhere.

"Teddy bear, teddy bear, turn around," Harriet chanted.

She spun her body to check what her cousins were up to. Their eyes kept darting to her. They were plotting something. She was determined not to be caught out.

"Enemy aircraft ahead!" Robert shouted.

"Attack!" Billy and Mickey shouted.

Billy jumped to his feet and ran at Harriet. He was fast for a six-year-old, and Harriet had to work hard to dodge around his outstretched arms.

"Leave me alone," Harriet said.

"The enemy is within range. Get ready to drop your bombs. Go! Go! Go!" Robert commanded.

Billy threw his body at Harriet, and Mickey copied. Each time they collided with her, the boys made bomb noises. Harriet stopped and folded her arms.

"I'm not playing," she said.

"We have a prisoner of war," Robert said. "Tie her up."

Billy grabbed Harriet by the arm while Mickey went to get the rope.

"No!" Harriet screamed. "I hate you. I hate your games. I hate this house. I hate this place. I want to go home." She jerked out of Billy's grasp. Her throat was tight, but there was no way she would cry.

She ran up the three wooden stairs, across the patio and burst through the kitchen door. She took in the scene as her eyes adjusted to the dim light. There was the doctor, stethoscope in hand, listening to her mother's chest. Harriet's Auntie Helen sat at the kitchen table with a cup of tea and Uncle Val stood, leaning on the mantelpiece of the unlit fireplace.

The rattling sound of her mother's breathing sounded worse than any enemy bombs. The clean Canadian air had not made her better.

"Run along and play," Auntie Helen said. "There's a good girl."

"I don't want to play their games," Harriet replied. "I want to stay here with Mummy." She stamped her foot on the kitchen floor.

"Ah, we're all coming to terms with not getting what we want in wartime," the doctor said. "I want to make medical history, find cures for all my patients but look at me, working as hard as ever while the junior doctors are off trying to keep soldiers alive. We all have to accept we can't have everything we want. What you need are some friends, some girls you can play with while you get used to your new life. Now, go outside and play. Your mother needs to rest."

Harriet returned to the yard, arms folded, shoulders slumped, and teeth clenched so tightly her jaw ached.

"Not so easy to get your own way here, is it?" Robert said, smirking from ear to ear.

Harriet walked past the three boys, straight for the back gate.

"Where do you think you're going?" Robert asked.

"Anywhere you aren't."

"You can't. We're not allowed to leave the yard without a grown-up," Robert said.

"You do."

"That's different. I go to the bakery, to work. If you want to carry sacks of flour and sweep floors, be my guest."

Harriet remembered the picnic they'd had by Loughlin Lake when they'd arrived. Was that only a week ago? The entire family, except her resting mother, carried rugs and hampers down a path, through the forest and set up by the water. The mountains towered over them as they drank lemonade, ate fruit-cake and swam in the murky water. *If I have to share a room with three boy cousins, at least I have this to escape to*, Harriet had thought to herself.

"Why can't we go to the lake?" Harriet asked.

"Because. It's. Not. Safe." Robert articulated every word.

"I used to live in London, during the war. A bomb fell in my schoolyard. What could be so dangerous here?"

"Cougars!" Mickey shouted.

He jumped to his feet and made clawing movements at Billy.

"Bears!" Billy squealed.

He stood up, reached high above his head, and took two bear steps towards Mickey. They pounced on each other, growling and fighting until Robert grabbed Mickey and Harriet held Billy.

"Stop fighting," Robert said. "Do you want Father to come out?"

Robert cuffed his brothers around their heads and turned to Harriet. "See what happens when you wind them up. Just do as you're told, or it'll be your fault they get in trouble."

"And who are you to order me around?" Harriet took two steps towards the back gate.

"You know, there's something much worse than bears and cougars in that forest," Robert said.

He walked to the Douglas fir, squatted down and placed his hands behind his back.

"What?" Harriet asked.

"Come over here and I'll tell you."

Harriet eyed her cousin suspiciously. She was sure she'd seen him pick up something in his hand.

"Why can't you tell me from there?"

"I don't want Billy and Mickey to get nightmares."

Robert had an answer for everything. Harriet longed to explore, to run free, without her uncle, aunt, mother or cousins watching her. She longed for time on her own and had to know why this was forbidden.

Harriet and Robert looked each other in the eyes.

"Don't you trust me?" Robert asked.

Everything inside her screamed "No! I don't trust you!" but something forced her forward.

"Closer," Robert said. "I have to whisper this in your ear."

Harriet leaned towards her cousin and placed a knee on the ground.

"Somewhere in these mountains lives a creature so huge and wild, it can rip a man apart with its bare hands."

She rolled her eyes. "That's a story told to scare little kids— like the bogeyman. I wasn't born yesterday," Harriet said.

"You don't believe me. Ask anyone in town and they'll tell you of the hunter who tried to protect himself from an attack. He shot the monster and twenty other monsters chased him down. They held him and chewed off his feet. Ignoring his screams, they yanked his legs from his body. The hunter died when they threw his arms to waiting cougars, and his entrails to the crows."

"How do you know? If he died, how did he tell the story?"

"His son watched the whole thing, hidden behind a tree."

"And what kind of monster did he see?"

"The smelly sasquatch!" Robert shouted.

Robert's hand shot out from behind his back. Harriet scrambled backward but couldn't get away. A leaf crumpled against her neck, and then soft, putrid raccoon poop was smeared across her face and down the front of her dress.

Victorious laughter burst out, and Harriet ran to the house.

"Mummy! Mummy! I hate him! I hate him! I hate him! We have to leave, now. I never want to see him again!"

Astonished adults stared at Harriet. Then Uncle Val took large, long strides across the kitchen, pushed open the fly-screen door and shouted, "Robert Edward Davis, go to your room. And on your way, choose which of my belts I am going to use."

# CHAPTER THREE
## HOMESICK

The next morning, Uncle Val sat at the head of the kitchen table with his army haircut, starched uniform and stern face. Harriet's mother sat, struggling for breath. She wore a thick, woollen cardigan despite the heat. Her skin was pale and looked paper thin. Her watery eyes struggled to stay open.

"Morning Mummy," Harriet said. She longed for the day her mother would look better. Today was not the day.

Billy and Mickey followed Harriet into the kitchen with their arms held out in front of them, walking stiffly and making weird ghost noises.

"She's a mummy. Come back from the dead," Billy said.

"Leave it," Uncle Val threatened.

The boys sat at the table in silence and gave Harriet an evil look. She tried to ignore them. Usually, she thought five- and six-year-old boys were the dumbest creatures on the planet but, looking at her mother, Harriet admitted they had a point. Her mother looked like a corpse, and their joke rammed a poker into her stomach. The long journey and constant noise in her cousins' house had made her mother sicker than ever. They needed to get their own place, wait until the war was over, then go home.

"Now, what's happened to your brother?" Auntie Helen chirped as she fussed around the cooker. "Robert, breakfast is ready."

There was no answer. The sound of pancakes frying on the griddle and the constant wheezing coming from Harriet's mother accompanied the silence.

"Robert! We're all waiting for you," Auntie Helen sung out.

Nothing. Where was he? The combination of the smell of boot polish and baking made Harriet want to barf. Her heart pounded in her chest. Why wouldn't he come when his mother called him? Robert seemed to try to make his father angry on the day he was leaving for war. He was asking for another licking and Harriet refused to care. In her mind, Robert deserved everything he got.

Uncle Val placed his enormous hands on the table and stood up. His broad, muscular frame seemed out of place in the small, cozy kitchen. He sighed audibly and took two giant strides across the room. Everyone froze. The boys glared at Harriet as if this was her fault. She gritted her teeth and stared back at them.

When Uncle Val reached the kitchen door, Robert breezed in.

"Sorry, I'm late. You should've started without me," he said. "I couldn't decide which shirt to wear to the parade."

"Oh, you silly," Auntie Helen said. "I told you, Sunday best. Never mind. Let's give thanks and eat before everything gets cold."

Uncle Val gave Robert a warning look, sat and said grace. Then mayhem broke out. Hands grabbed at the maple syrup, knives scraped across plates, forks stabbed at the extra pancakes in the middle of the table and mouths chewed contentedly. Robert looked at Harriet and smirked. She looked away and saw her mother's untouched food. Then she spotted Uncle Val's army photo on the mantlepiece next to her father's.

This was all wrong. Harriet didn't belong here. Her father's photo belonged above the fireplace in the officer's quarters in

Greenwich. They had forced her from her home and made her move in with this rabble. If her father were here, they'd move into their own house. She wouldn't have to share a room with three cousins, and he'd know how to make her mother well again. Her eyes prickled. She bit the inside of her lip to stop herself from crying.

"May I leave the table?" she said.

"Of course, dear," Auntie Helen said. "Have you had enough to eat?"

Harriet nodded her head, afraid any more words would make her cry. She rushed from the room and climbed onto her bunk bed. From under her pillow, she took a framed photo of her father and the envelope containing his letter. She hugged them both to her chest as tears poured down her face.

"Oh Daddy," she cried. "Come and rescue me, please. I need you."

She looked at the photo and remembered her father sitting in his favourite chair, smoking a pipe. In Greenwich, whenever Harriet came into the sitting room, he'd look over his shoulder and smile with his whole face. He'd stand as she ran to him, greeted her with outstretched arms and swung her into an embrace. "How's my princess?" he'd ask, holding her so tight it was hard to breathe. Then when he relaxed his grip, a tingle would start in the pit of her stomach and radiate through her entire body. But he was not here to hold her.

"Oh Daddy, make the war end. Mummy and I need our own place. I can't live here. Please come and rescue me. You promised you would."

She searched for answers as she stared at the photo in her hands. Her father's frozen smile stared back at her. She touched the photo frame and longed to remember the feel of his skin. Harriet opened and reread the letter. She tried to hear her father's voice, but the only sound in her head was hers. She remembered sitting in his lap as he told her about faraway lands and marvellous adventures. But she'd changed so much since he left. Now, her long legs would dangle awkwardly if she tried to sit on his lap.

"You said I'd be happy here. You said Mummy would feel better. You said there are forests, lakes and mountains. And there are, but I can't explore them. Nothing you said is true. I hate my cousins. Mummy is sicker than ever. Will you ever join us here?"

Harriet stopped herself. Her father had to survive the war. He had to come back to her. If her father were here, she wouldn't have to stay in the yard. She'd go on adventures and no one would stop her.

Uncle Val's voice broke into her daydream. "Time to go. Leave the dishes. Today of all days I can't be late."

Harriet dried her tears. Placed the letter carefully into its envelope, tucked it behind the photo frame and placed them both carefully under her pillow.

She joined her aunt, uncle and cousins as they clambered into shoes and coats.

"What's all the fuss," Harriet mumbled. "The King and news cameras won't be here like Daddy's farewell."

# CHAPTER FOUR
## THE MAN OF THE HOUSE

Uncle Val took long strides as he walked the two blocks to the town centre. Robert tried to imitate him, but his gangly legs made him look like a clown on stilts. Auntie Helen, Billy and Mickey were almost running to keep up. Harriet hung back, smiling at how ridiculous they looked until her thoughts drifted to her mother. She'd stayed at home, unable to manage the short walk to town. Panic started as an empty feeling in Harriet's gut and threatened to engulf her body. What if her mother didn't recover? Would she live with Robert forever? That couldn't happen. There had to be a cure somewhere. Someone had to know how to get her mother better.

Harriet's thoughts jolted back to the present at the sound of her uncle's voice.

"Morning, Kieran, morning, Mrs. McLoughlin," Uncle Val said. "Pleasant weather for the parade."

The woman in front of Harriet had a fierce red mark on her swollen face. The man next to her wore an army uniform and a grim expression. Harriet couldn't take her eyes off the woman and wondered why no one asked her about the bruise turning from red to purple as they stood talking about the weather.

There were children everywhere. They ran around and waved

flags. One boy sung "It's a Long Way to Tipperary." Another joined in, then shouted, "Dad, are you going to kill Hitler?"

"Let's not talk about killing today," Kieran McLoughlin said. "But someone had better warn Hitler, Mussolini and Emperor Hirohito that a McLoughlin is coming to get them."

With that, the huge, broad-shouldered man jumped off the porch and chased three boys with wild red hair. Billy and Mickey joined in. Harriet felt relieved when she saw a smile spread over Mrs. McLoughlin's face. Then she noticed a girl about her own age with a baby in her arms. The girl's eyes drilled into Harriet's and willed her to stop staring at her mother. Harriet averted her gaze. She'd been told many times that staring was rude, but Harriet couldn't stop. She wanted to know what wasn't being said, and hoped, if she watched carefully enough, it would fill the gaps in the conversation. Auntie Helen saw the two girls looking at each other.

"Harriet," Auntie Helen said. "This is Annie. How old are you now, dear? You're all growing up too quickly."

"Twelve, Mrs. Davis."

"Twelve and look at how good you are with your baby brother. Harriet, Annie will teach you how to look after little uns while us moms have to work."

"Someone has to teach her how to do something useful," Robert mumbled.

Uncle Val raised a hand in the air and silenced Robert with a look.

Harriet took two steps towards Annie and held out her hand.

"Nice to meet you," Harriet said.

Annie transferred the baby from one hip to the other so she could shake hands. Harriet saw oatmeal smeared on the front of Annie's dress. From below, a grubby hand grabbed the hem on Harriet's neatly ironed skirt. Harriet yanked the material from the child and turned up her nose.

The two families melted together. Mr. McLoughlin and the

young boys ran on ahead. The mothers chatted nervously about the weather and food prices, and Robert walked next to his stepfather. Annie held the baby in one arm and walked hand in hand with a sister. Harriet smiled in Annie's direction but kept her distance. She'd counted. The McLoughlins had six children. What would she have in common with someone from such a big family?

As they turned the corner onto Main Street, Harriet guffawed. There was nothing "main" about a town with one church, six shops and a pub. Harriet remembered her own father's farewell with hundreds of well-wishers lining London streets, waving Union Jacks as they watched the King inspect the troops.

No one of significance lived in Loughlin. In England, her father's men were in crisp, white naval uniforms. Here, the men wore dull khaki and stood in small family groups.

Harriet looked around. Across the road, a man was scrubbing the remains of a swastika from his shop window. Billy and Mickey saw it as well, and goose-stepped like German soldiers.

"I'll have none of that," Auntie Helen said, cuffing the boys around their ears. "Herr Schmidt is one of us. He has been serving this town for twenty years. It's terrible the way some people are treating him."

Robert kicked his feet in the dust at the side of the road and said, "He's probably a spy."

"You read too much," Uncle Val said.

"And only the sheriff can say if there's wrongdoing," Auntie Helen replied. "It's bad enough the poor man has to report to the police every week like he's a criminal. This is his home and you'll treat him as one of us."

Harriet stepped aside and watched the kaleidoscope of people milling around. On her own, she could inch closer to the man scrubbing at the graffiti, listen in to conversations, and see if anyone else thought he was a spy. She found the notion of espionage in this tiny town both fascinating and ridiculous.

"I haven't seen you around here before."

A man in a brown suit held out his hand. He had a camera hanging from a leather strap around his neck and a label on his hat. It read "press." Harriet looked at her aunt and uncle. They were deep in conversation. Harriet felt uneasy talking to a grown-up, but swallowed her nervousness, and shook hands. Her father always told her to lock any shyness inside and pretend confidence whenever necessary.

"I'm Harriet Hall."

"Al Gunner, editor of *The Three Mills Gazette*."

Harriet had never heard an adult use their first name when introducing themselves to a child. Harriet stood taller. She must look older and more important than she felt. The man took out a notebook, licked the end of a pencil and asked, "Miss Hall, what brings you here today?"

"My uncle has volunteered. He leaves today."

"Good for him. It doesn't sound as if you come from around here."

Harriet stuck out her chin and said proudly, "No. I'm from London. My father's a captain in the British Royal Navy."

"I'm honoured to meet someone so important."

"What do you write about?" Harriet asked. "I love stories, but surely nothing happens around here."

"Oh, you'd be surprised. Keep your eyes peeled. Newsworthy snippets happen everywhere. You just need to have a nose for them."

"Harriet," Auntie Helen called. "Come over here. The parade is about to start."

Harriet watched the newspaper editor shuffle across the road and sidle up to a group of men standing outside The Coach and Horses. He arranged them into a group, took their photo, then stood with his notebook. Harriet wanted to listen to the interview, but Auntie Helen grabbed her by the hand and dragged her back to their family group.

Uncle Val hugged his wife and ruffled the hair on Billy's and

Mickey's heads. Auntie Helen grabbed the small boys and held them tightly. She blinked quickly and forced her lips together. Harriet watched her aunt swallow her tears, determined not to cry as her husband turned to his stepson.

"You're the man of the house now," Uncle Val said. "Take care of everyone for me."

Uncle Val took a step towards his wife. He kissed Billy and Mickey on the tops of their heads, brushed a single tear away from Auntie Helen's cheek, turned and coughed loudly. His deep resonant voice cut through a hundred private moments.

"Fall in!" he commanded.

The women and children shuffled back. A khaki line marched down the road, past the shops until they reached army trucks waiting outside the church. The men climbed on board, the engines started, and the men disappeared down the road. Billy and Mickey waved their flags above their heads. Auntie Helen handed a handkerchief to Mrs. McLoughlin. Harriet watched as Annie's mother wiped away a tear and winced as she touched a bruise on her cheek.

"Be strong, Milly," Auntie Helen said. "We'll all help each other. Won't we, Harriet?"

Harriet looked at her aunt, then at Mrs. McLoughlin. Something was going on. Something was not being said. Harriet heard a car door open. She looked to see Al Gunner get into his car. He had seen her as she watched the mothers. He tapped the side of his nose. Harriet knew she had smelled out a story. Her stomach churned and her body shuddered. There were some stories Harriet didn't want to find out about.

A cry drew Harriet's attention to Annie and the children swarming around her knees. One child was picking his nose and examining the bogie on his finger. Harriet watched as Annie flicked the hand from the child's mouth, picked up a foil chocolate wrapper from the ground, tucked it into her pocket and picked up the screaming child. Harriet felt sick to her stomach. She would not look after someone else's brothers and sisters. It was not her job. The McLoughlins needed a nanny or house-keeper to clean these kids and teach them manners.

These thoughts, and so many more, flooded through Harriet's mind. Then, Robert edged closer to her with a smirk across his face. He whispered, "I know what you're thinking, Harriet Hall. You're a snob. You think you're better than us."

"I'm better than you," Harriet said.

"That's as may be, but I'm in charge now. You heard Father. I'm the man of the house, so you have to follow my orders. You'll regret the day you squealed on Robert Edward Davis."

He crossed his arms and sneered at Harriet until her blood boiled.

# CHAPTER FIVE
## PRESS PASS

The dust from the army trucks hadn't settled before Robert sauntered to his mother's side, took off his jacket and tie and undid his top button.

"Can Annie and I go to Brennan this afternoon? There's a new movie showing, we've both got enough aluminium to get in free and I've got money for popcorn," Robert said.

"Take your cousin with you," Auntie Helen said.

"But Mom," Robert said.

"No buts. You either take Harriet or stay in Loughlin."

Robert took a deep breath and looked at Annie. Something in his eyes told Harriet he didn't want her to go with them. Harriet looked from her cousin to Annie. If Robert didn't want her in Brennan, then that was where she would be. In her head, she argued with herself. She told herself that she could enjoy some peace and quiet on her own, but her heart wanted to get out of town, be with kids and forget about her mother. The movies would be fun, she told herself.

"We could go to Cullen Mills railway station on the way. See if the soldiers dropped more chocolate wrappers. I bet we could find enough for Harriet's ticket," Annie said.

"No, no, no," Mrs. McLoughlin said. "You girls are too

young to be hanging around railway stations. What if the train was delayed? Young girls and soldiers, it's just not right."

"I agree," Auntie Helen said. "You go straight to Brennan. Watch the movie and come straight back. You can use your popcorn money on Harriet's ticket."

"That is so unfair," Robert said.

Harriet didn't see what the problem was, but she wouldn't argue. She followed Robert and Annie to the bakery. Robert stormed inside, came out with three bread rolls, tossed one to Annie and threw the other at Harriet. Then, he collected the shop's delivery bike with its heavy black frame and gigantic breadbasket. He wheeled it back to Annie's house, where she grabbed her own bike.

"How am I going to get there?" Harriet asked.

Robert pointed to the basket on the front of the bike.

"You're kidding me!" Harriet said.

"Or you can run? Whichever takes your fancy," Robert said.

Harriet looked from Robert to Annie, climbed into the basket and sulked.

Robert pedaled hard as they rode out of town. Dust flew into Harriet's eyes. She wanted to lift her hand and protect her face but didn't dare let go of the basket. She hung on tight and bounced from side to side. Could Robert make her more uncomfortable? She knew Robert wanted her to give up, ask him to stop and let her walk back to Loughlin. This made her determined to put up with the bumps and scratches without complaining. Mountains towered on either side until they reached the crossroad leading out of town. Harriet glanced over her shoulder. Beads of sweat ran down Robert's face and neck. He looked at Annie. Harriet smiled to herself. At that moment Harriet realized Robert liked Annie and the more she knew about someone, the more power she had over them.

"I don't know what you're smiling about," Robert said. "You're cycling home."

The road opened to flat farmland. Row after row of plants

filled the fields. The wind blew through Harriet's hair as she sat and plotted how she could get the upper hand over Robert. If she became friends with Annie, Robert would have to do what she wanted, or she'd turn Annie away from him.

A car horn jolted Harriet from her thoughts.

"You look like you could do with some help."

Al Gunner, the reporter, wound down his window and squinted at the three children on two bikes.

"Where are you off to?" he said.

"Brennan," Robert replied.

"Then jump in, Miss Hall. That's where my office is, and I have this morning's parade to write up."

Harriet clambered out of the basket and climbed into the Vauxhall Beetle. She felt giddy with excitement. Al Gunner had offered her a lift and left Robert and Annie to cycle the rest of the way. Harriet wound down her window, waved to Annie and watched as her companions disappeared in a cloud of dust.

As they sped along the road, Harriet stared out the window, taking in her unfamiliar surroundings, answering questions about her father's naval command and her move to Canada. The farmland switched to housing and then shops. They had taken all signs down to confuse invading Japanese or German armies. Harriet assumed they were entering Brennan, one of the three mill towns they named the gazette after. The town was bigger than Loughlin. Harriet counted two churches, a school, fifteen shops, several offices and a movie theatre. Mr. Gunner pulled up outside one of the wooden buildings with The Three Mills Gazette painted on the siding.

"Why is there a mill so far from the forest?" Harriet asked.

"What?"

"Brennan Mills is in the middle of farmland."

"Oh, you're sharp."

Harriet's chest filled with pride. She was sharp and much brighter than her cousin, who was sweating somewhere on the road between the two towns.

"You have a journalistic sense for questions," Mr. Gunner said. "They cleared the forest for crops long before I was born, long before my father was born. Now, even the paper mill has moved to Cullen Mills, so it's near the railway. They'll stay busy. In wartime everyone wants news, and the printing press waits for no one."

Al Gunner raised his hat and opened his office door.

"Enjoy your movie. Have you got your ball of foil?"

Harriet looked blank.

"A handful of aluminium foil will get you in for free," Mr. Gunner said. "I saw your friend collecting hers."

Harriet crossed her arms and fumed silently. That was why Annie collected garbage from the ground. Now she understood why Annie and Robert were keen to make sure they had collected enough. It would've been kind if someone had explained that to her. Instead, Robert had to use his popcorn money. She'd be in Robert's debt or be left outside the theatre. Either way, Robert would have the upper hand. Harriet pictured Robert's smug smile and her stomach swirled in fury.

"Tell you what," Mr. Gunner said. "You can do me a favour. I'll give you my press pass. Watch *The Trial*. I have to cover a court case next week. You can take the movie version; I'll do the real thing. Enjoy your afternoon, then write a one-hundred-word review. If you like writing, it can be your first assignment. Think you're up to it?"

He disappeared inside and returned with a notebook, pen and pass.

"One hundred words on my desk by Wednesday."

With that, he handed Harriet the tools of his trade, turned and walked inside. Harriet looked down at her hand, not sure how she'd landed a job writing in the summer holidays.

Robert and Annie cycled up to the movie theatre. They pulled out their balls of foil. Robert exchanged his for a ticket.

"Is this enough for two tickets?" Annie asked.

The man in the booth looked doubtful.

"Don't worry," Harriet said. "I have a pass."

She flashed the card and was waved into the theatre. Robert tried to cover his astonishment, but Harriet saw the jealousy in his eyes as she strode into the theatre. Annie and Robert followed her in.

After two hours, the three children burst out into the late afternoon sunshine.

"That was brilliant," Annie said.

"I knew the husband was lying," Robert said.

"But wasn't the lawyer amazing," Annie continued.

"He did his job," Robert said.

"Putting the child on the witness stand, what a twist," Harriet said. "Who would have thought of that? Then, he got the child to tell the courtroom the truth about her mother committing murder. Brilliant! It goes to show how much more us kids know than adults give us credit for."

"Are you writing that in your review?" Robert said. "Twelve-year-old Harriet Hall says, 'Watch out parents, your children know more than you think they know.'"

"You're jealous because someone asked me to write the review, not you."

"I think you'll do a great job. I know I'd read a review written by a kid," Annie said.

Harriet blushed with pride. She was going to write the best review in the world. She ran across the road, handed the press card back to Mr. Gunner and thanked him for the opportunity.

"See you Wednesday," Mr. Gunner said.

Harriet jumped in the breadbasket and took out her note-book and pencil. All the way back she made notes as the bike bounced over the rough road.

She felt the warm afternoon sun and saw their long shadows dance along the road as the mountains around Loughlin came nearer. Maybe she could survive the war, investigating and writing stories. If only she could get out into the mountains and experience the adventures her father promised.

# CHAPTER SIX
## BASEBALL

The next morning, Harriet woke to the sounds of Billy and Mickey climbing onto Robert's bunk.

"Get off," Robert said. "Go jump on Harry. I have to get to the bakery."

"It's Harriet."

"If you sleep in the boy's room, you get treated like a boy," Robert replied.

Billy and Mickey climbed down from Robert's bunk, stumbled across the room and up another ladder to Harriet's bed. They giggled and chanted, "Harry, Harry."

Harriet pulled the covers up to her chin as the boys jumped on her. Billy took Harriet's braids and handed one to Mickey. They bounced up and down shouting, "Gee up, Horse Harry." And "Ride 'em, cowboy."

"Get off me!" Harriet screamed. "Mummy, Mummy."

Auntie Helen came to the bedroom door.

"Billy and Mickey get down from there this instant. I've no time or patience for these shenanigans. I've been up since four. I'm only here to get breakfast and check Robert's awake. I still have two dozen loaves to bake before we open. Now, breakfast is ready. Robert, we leave in ten minutes."

Robert climbed down his ladder, grabbed his flour-covered overalls and wandered to the bathroom. Auntie Helen moved closer to Harriet and wiped a tear from her cheek.

"Try to let your mother rest and don't let these little rascals get to you. You'll soon get used to them," Auntie Helen said. "The bakery closes at noon today. Help to look after your cousins 'til then, and perhaps we can take a picnic down to the lake this afternoon. Pull on your dressing gown and slippers. You'll feel better after you've eaten. Come on, if you're not fast, they'll eat everything."

Harriet buried her head under the blankets and prayed she'd wake up from this nightmare. She wanted her old bed in her own bedroom. She even missed the noise of London traffic and the smell of smog. She wanted her mom to be well and her dad to hug her pain away. She needed to get away from her cousins, to be on her own, to explore the forests she'd marveled at from the train. None of this was possible. No one asked her what she liked or wanted to do. Her eyes stung and her stomach churned. Everything had changed. Harriet longed to turn back time and erase Loughlin from her life.

"You heard Mother," Robert said. "You're looking after Billy and Mickey this morning."

"They're your brothers. You should do it."

"Half-brothers and I have to work in the bakery."

"I'll swap."

"You! You're a girl!"

"So!"

"Robert, Harriet, come and eat breakfast," Auntie Helen called. "And stop arguing."

"After you," Robert said. "And don't forget to make your bed."

Harriet stomped to the kitchen. She hated the way Robert always had the last word.

Robert sat opposite her, cut a huge chunk of bread and smothered it in butter. Every time he did this, Harriet expected him to be told off. In London, butter was rationed. There was beef dripping, but Harriet preferred to eat dry toast. Butter was a rare treat. Harriet took a tiny knob of butter and scraped it on a thin slice of bread. She'd show the Davis family the proper way to live through a war. Then Auntie Helen took an equally enormous amount of butter and put it on her bread. Harriet was disgusted by the excess. Oblivious to Harriet's feelings, Auntie Helen picked up her breakfast, covered her hair with a scarf and walked to the door. "Robert, time to go," Auntie Helen said. "Have a good morning, stay in the yard and Harriet, be a good girl, try to let your mother sleep. The doctor said rest is vital."

"You heard what Mother said. Be a good girl," Robert said.

Harriet sat in stunned silence. Billy had strawberry jam smeared across his face and Mickey ate with his mouth open. Gross! She got up from the table and walked to her mother's room. She tapped on the door and pushed it open.

The curtains were still closed. It took time for Harriet's eyes to adjust to the dim light. Her mother's eyes opened slowly. Her ghostly skin molded into the pillow, her wheezing cut fear into Harriet's heart, and the smell of menthol pushed Harriet away.

"Come here, my precious one," Harriet's mom said.

"How are you feeling?" Harriet asked.

"Better," Harriet's mom said.

Harriet noticed her mother's eyes didn't meet her gaze. She could tell her mother was lying.

"We're going on a picnic later. Can you come?"

Harriet's heart ached. Her throat tightened, and she swallowed back the tears. She knew the answer before her mom's dry lips moved.

"Maybe next time my love."

"Harriet! Harriet!" Billy and Mickey shouted. "Where are you?"

"Go and play. I'll be better soon, and you can show me all the places you've discovered."

Harriet left with a heavy heart, dressed, threw her bedspread over her unmade bed and took her cousins outside so her mother could rest.

"All the places I've discovered?" Harried mumbled. "Chance'd be a fine thing. Stuck in this yard with these two."

"What d'you want to play?" Billy asked.

"Nothing."

Harriet picked up a baseball and threw it against the Douglas fir. It hit the tree with a thud and fell to the ground.

"You can't even play D.O.N.K.E.Y. with this," Harriet moaned and thought of the ball games she'd played with her friends in London.

"Let's play," Billy said.

Billy and Mickey ran to the shed, got the bat and mitts.

"Harriet, you pitch first," Billy said. "I'll bat. Mickey, you be catcher."

Billy measured his batting distance from an imaginary home base. Mickey stood like the wicket keeper of the officers cricket team. Harriet took the ball, swung her straight arm behind her back, over her shoulder and released the ball. It bounced before reaching Billy, then flew back and hit the tree.

"Howzat!" Harriet shouted. "You're out!"

"Am not! And what was that?"

The boys laughed and copied Harriet's bowling.

"It's called cricket, and I never said I wanted to play," Harriet said, and her face flushed red

She stormed off, took her jump rope and threw it over a Douglas fir branch. The boys looked on in awe as Harriet held the rope, placed her feet on the trunk and scaled the tree.

"That's cool," Billy said. "Show us, show us, show us."

Mickey joined in the chant until Harriet climbed down and showed the boys how to climb the tree.

Eventually, Auntie Helen and Robert got home. Flour covered Robert's clothes, hair and face.

"Woooo!" Harriet said.

Billy and Mickey laughed and ran around the yard, pretending to be ghosts.

"You should lift flour sacks all morning," Robert complained. "See if you like it."

"Don't tease him," Auntie Helen said. "Robert, dust yourself down outside. Then wash. I'll make sandwiches. We've just seen Mrs. McLoughlin and we're all going to the lake for that picnic."

"Can't I stay and read?" Robert asked.

"No! It's your turn to look after your brothers," Harriet said.

"Half-brothers," Robert said.

"No more about that," Auntie Helen chirped. "You can bring your book with you. The fresh air will do you good."

Robert stormed into the house, slamming the door behind him. Two seconds later, the door flew open again.

"Harriet, you're the laziest girl on the planet. Make your bed."

"Oh Harriet, haven't you done that yet?" Auntie Helen asked. "It needs to be done before the picnic."

Resentment bubbled inside Harriet as she stormed up the steps. Inside, her bedspread was on the floor and the ruffled bedding was on display for all to see. Back in London, someone made her bed by the time she climbed into it. She didn't know if her mom or Mrs. Peters made it. She'd never thought about it before. It was just something that happened.

Harriet struggled to straighten the sheets and blankets on her top bunk. Robert came in from the bathroom, looking clean in his shorts and t-shirt.

"Glad to see you doing as you're told," Robert said. "You're learning who's the boss around here."

Harriet watched him leave the room, hit her pillow with her fist and picked it up. Her photo frame and letter were missing. She tossed the pillows aside, looked in the dresser and toy box. It wasn't under the bed. Nothing. Panic gripped her body. She wanted to double over and hold her aching stomach. Instead, she stood tall, shook with rage and ran to the yard. Robert was sitting in the tree.

"Give them back," Harriet shouted.

Harriet had never been in a fight before but, at that moment, she wished she could reach her cousin. She wanted to pound his smug face with her fists, kick his stomach until it felt as tight and sore as hers, and tear his thieving hands from his body.

"What? These?"

Robert waved Harriet's treasures above his head. Then he read from the letter, "My darling princess."

"Don't! They're mine. That letter's private. Give them back."

Harriet tightened every muscle in her body, crossed her arms and stamped her foot. Her tears were about to erupt and as soon as they did, Harriet knew she'd lose.

"My beautiful angel."

"I hate you Robert Edward Davis," Harriet cried.

"Cry baby bunting, daddy's gone a hunting," Robert chanted.

"Give them back or else," Harriet screamed.

"Or, or, or else…"

Harriet burst into tears and ran into the house. "Mummy, Mummy, we have to move. I can't live with him."

Harriet opened the door to her mother's bedroom. Harriet's mother opened her eyes and smiled vacantly. Auntie Helen put her hands on Harriet's shoulders, turned her away from the room and closed the door.

"Let your mother rest. I know the boys can be a bit much, but you'll get used to them. Come on, you can play with Annie this afternoon."

"I want the things Robert stole from me or I'm not going."

Auntie Helen sighed. "I've told him to put them back."

Harriet grunted. She couldn't believe how much Robert got away with now her uncle had left for war.

"Harriet, a word of advice," Auntie Helen said. "Don't let

him know they're important to you. It makes you vulnerable. Act as if you don't care and he'll lose interest."

Harriet wiped the tears from her face as she stood in the kitchen watching Auntie Helen packing the last few picnic things. As they left the house, Harriet allowed the noise and bustle to fill the growing space inside her—a hole gnawed away with the unspoken fear of her mother dying.

# CHAPTER SEVEN
## PICNIC

The air was stifling as they walked the few steps to the McLoughlins' house. Harriet hung back and watched as Billy and Mickey became a tumbling mass of limbs with Annie's brothers and sister. They were like the chimpanzee enclosure at London Zoo, gangly arms and legs all over each other. One child would make a break for it, and then others would chase him down. They tumbled on lawns and jumped over hedges. The youngest ape creature clung to Annie. That Annie had gotten to the movie theatre without a child fixed to her hip amazed Harriet. This baby seemed to be a permanent fixture. There was no way she could skip, explore, or even jump in the lake with a baby in her arms. Annie smiled at Harriet and fell into step beside her. Harriet shuddered. She and Annie looked like mini versions of the adults, walking down the road. Harriet longed to return to the lasso tossing, rule breaking, wild child of Greenwich.

Harriet looked around. Robert stared at Annie from a distance. He looked away when he realized Harriet had seen him. This confirmed in Harriet's mind that Robert liked Annie. Harriet looked to Annie, who giggled and turned red. Annie also liked Robert and knew he liked her. This was too much for

Harriet. She couldn't understand how anyone could like Robert.

Panic gripped Harriet's heart. If Robert and Annie were friends, she had no one. She looked around; she wanted Robert to be the odd one out. Then, as if by silent agreement, Robert broke into a run and Annie raced to catch up to him. They led the way down a short, steep path leading into the forest. Harriet wondered how she could feel so alone with all these people around her. She told herself she didn't care, but Harriet wanted to make her own discoveries, far away from the constant chatter of a family picnic. Every kid had a mom with them, except her. Harriet's chest tightened as loose stones seemed to shift under her feet. Twice Harriet had to put a hand to the ground to stop from falling. When she looked up, Robert was squatting and had a group of children around him.

"That's raccoon poop," he said. "You can tell by the purplish mound with fruit pits showing. You know all about this, don't you, Harry?" He smirked.

All the children laughed. Even Annie covered her mouth to hide her giggle. Harriet's humiliation was complete. Everyone knew she'd fallen for the "Smelly Sasquatch" joke. She hated him and couldn't wait to get even.

Robert led the way, stopping to point out trees, the difference between deer and rabbit poop. He found frogs under logs, hairy caterpillars on leaves; he drew everyone's attention to bear claw marks on a fallen log.

Harriet looked and listened. Robert seemed to know a lot about the forest. She hadn't thought he was smart enough to learn so much from books.

"They use their claws to rip open the bark and get to the bugs inside," Robert said. "And they'll rip you in two if you're here on your own."

Robert reached up high, made his hands into bear paws and chased the screaming gaggle down the path. Annie smiled towards Harriet.

"He's so clever," Annie said.

"Who?"

"Robert."

"Robert?"

"He's always the top in class. I wish I knew half the stuff he does."

Harriet didn't see Uncle Val as a naturalist.

"Who taught him?" Harriet asked.

"He's always in the library. Always reading. He wants to be a teacher like his real dad, but my mom says he'll have to run the bakery, at least until the war is over. It's a shame. I'd like school if he was my teacher."

Harriet and Annie walked the rest of the way in silence, each lost in her own thoughts. It never occurred to Harriet there would be books about animal poop. If he found out all this stuff in the library, Harriet wondered how he knew where everything was along the trail. Robert must break the rules and come here alone. Harriet thought about all the things Annie had said. She'd never heard about Robert's ambition to be a teacher. Harriet felt confused. Annie genuinely admired Robert. How was that possible? He was simply the most annoying boy Harriet had ever met.

When they reached the lake, they spread lunch out on a rug. At first, hungry hands grabbed at the sandwiches, biscuits and fruit. Then the moms sat swishing the flies away, watching children leap from the pier into the lake, dig holes in the dark sand and play by the water's edge.

Harriet soon tired of the noise. She slipped on her shoes, took a cheese sandwich and wandered back along the forest path. Her heart pounded in her chest as she imagined wild animals jumping out and attacking her.

"Don't be crazy," she said to herself. "Robert makes stories up."

She calmed herself and listened to the breeze rustling in the trees. The hair on the back of her neck bristled. Something was watching her. She turned slowly and let her eyes follow the tree trunk behind her. The hammering of a woodpecker made her jump and startled a squirrel clinging to the bark.

"I'm sorry," Harriet said. "I didn't mean to frighten you. Here, have some bread."

Harriet broke off a tiny piece of crust and threw it to the ground by the tree. The squirrel scuttled down the trunk, took the crumb, ran back into the tree, held the offering in its front paws and ate. The second piece of bread landed closer to Harriet. She wondered whether the squirrel would get close enough to her to stroke his long fluffy tail. In London, Harriet had gotten ducks to walk right up to her. She placed the third piece by her feet. A nut landed next to it. Harriet looked around. Her heartbeat quickened.

"Who's there?"

No one answered. Goosebumps covered her arms. There was a rustle in the thick undergrowth and then silence. Harriet's body froze but her mind started to race. Part of her wanted to run back to the picnic but she refused to give in. She had every right to explore this forest. Harriet took a deep breath, stood tall and decided to stay. Whatever it was, it had not pounced on her. She breathed a sigh of relief and nearly choked on the putrid smell.

"Well, whoever you are, you need a bath."

Harriet squatted down on the ground, watched and waited for the squirrel. It inched forward and Harriet stretched out her hand, holding the remains of the sandwich. The squirrel looked from the crumb to the nut to the bread in Harriet's hand, uncertain which to go for. Finally, he chose the nut and held it in his front paws to eat.

"Oh, you prefer forest food, do you?" Harriet said. "I'll have to call you Nutty."

She reached out her hand to stroke the midnight black fur. As her fingers stretched out, a hairy hand stretched its fingers towards the sandwich. Harriet's eyes followed the hand up a long hairy arm. When their eyes met, Harriet saw an enormous hairy face, not quite human, not quite animal staring, back at her. Harriet froze. She couldn't run away even if she'd wanted to. Her legs felt like jelly and the forest seemed to spin around her. All Harriet could focus on was the enormous beast staring at her. Harriet swallowed hard to make sure a scream didn't come out. She was staring at the smelly sasquatch. A creature who tore hunters apart. The beast tilted its head and raised its protruding eyebrows. The corner of its mouth raised in a half smile. Quick as a wink, the creature snatched Harriet's sandwich and retreated into the forest.

"Don't go," Harriet said.

Harriet felt something whistle past her ear. A rock skimmed the ground and hit Nutty. The squirrel bounded into the safety of the forest, and Harriet stood to confront the attacker.

Robert stood near the clearing. He threw another stone up into the air and caught it in his right hand.

"You shouldn't feed wild animals," he said.

"Then we shouldn't feed you," Harriet replied.

Harriet looked into the trees. The smiling face was gone. She wanted to brag about what she'd seen, but knew Robert wouldn't believe her. She decided this was going to be her secret.

"They get too used to humans. Forget how to fend for themselves. You'll be the death of them."

"And you'll be the death of me," Harriet grumbled.

"Come on, we're going home. Haven't you heard us calling for you?" Robert asked. He called over his shoulder towards the beach. "I've found her. She's over here."

Annie appeared and tried to hug Harriet.

"Get off me!" Harriet yelled. "Your boyfriend tried to kill a squirrel."

Annie looked at Robert, who rolled his eyes and made a circling motion at the side of his head. Harriet's anger bubbled and boiled inside her.

"Just ignore him," Annie said. "Boys can be really stupid."

But Harriet wouldn't even speak. She'd made friends with a

squirrel and seen a sasquatch. She was better than Robert and Annie put together. Feeling superior, she kicked stones along the forest path. She'd made a decision.

When they reached the Davis' home, Harriet went straight to her mother's room.

"Mummy, we're moving. I don't care where, but I'm not..." Harriet said, opening the bedroom door.

Harriet's mother did not move. Harriet felt blood drain from her face as her stomach dropped to the floor.

"Mummy! Mummy! Auntie Helen, Mummy's not moving!"

Auntie Helen ran to the bed and cupped her sister-in-law's cheek in her palm.

"Robert, run and get Dr. Smith. We need him here now!"

# CHAPTER EIGHT
## HOSPITAL

Two hospital orderlies lifted Harriet's mother into the back of the ambulance. Harriet tried to follow, but a hand on her shoulder stopped her.

"Hospitals are no place for children," Dr. Smith said. "Come along at visiting time. We'll have your mother feeling much better in no time."

"No! I want to be with her now!"

"Listen to the doctor," Auntie Helen said. "I'll go with her. Stay here and help Robert."

Auntie Helen climbed into the back of the ambulance, the doors closed, and they took Harriet's mother away, closely followed by the doctor in his Chrysler New Yorker.

Harriet stood frozen to the spot.

"Come on," Robert said. "Let's go in."

"I have to be with my mom."

"I know," Robert said. He looked at Harriet with sad, kind eyes, but she wouldn't be comforted by her cousin.

"How can you know? You know nothing!"

Harriet ran into the house, went straight to her bed and wept into her pillow. She reached under her pillow, found the photo and letter, and wondered when Robert had put her things back. She wiped the tears from her eyes and read her dad's letter for the hundredth time.

"'You will be happy there. You have three cousins to play with. The air is clean. Your mother will feel better.' That's a lie," Harriet cried. "All lies."

Robert walked quietly into the bedroom.

"They told me the same thing when they took my dad to hospital. He wasn't breathing, doctors took him away, and the next thing I knew he was dead."

Harriet sat in disbelief. Her mother couldn't die. Her tears stopped and her heart echoed in the cavern of her body. She had to see her mom.

"I know a way into the hospital," Robert continued. "If Annie will look after Billy and Mickey, I'll show you."

Harriet couldn't believe what she'd heard. Robert was offering to help her. Suspicion got buried under a sea of gratitude.

"I want to come," Billy said.

"Me too," Mickey added.

"Not this time," Robert said. "I'll take you on your own adventure when we get back."

A few minutes later, Harriet and Robert left the complaining boys with Annie, walked through town, picked up a breadbasket from the family bakery, covered it with a cloth and continued to Loughlin Memorial Hospital.

There was a long gravel driveway leading to the imposing red brick building. A nurse was pushing an old man in a wheelchair along one of the garden paths. Robert pulled Harriet behind a rhododendron bush and held his finger to his lips. Then the two children ran across the grass, around the main building and reached a courtyard. There, Harriet saw garbage bins lined up neatly against one wall. No one was in sight. Empty wooden crates were arranged in small groups. This was the place where staff gathered for their breaks. It reminded Harriet of the courtyard behind the Greenwich

Naval College—a place where she was in charge, where she led the way.

Robert strode towards the noise of the kitchen. A giant of a man in a white chef's outfit pushed the door open and looked down at him.

"What are you doing here today?" the chef asked.

"We had a call, asking if we had any more bread," Robert lied.

"I didn't order any. What have you got?"

"Just a couple of loaves. We don't bake on Saturday afternoon. It's all we had left."

"Take it inside. I'll pay you on Monday."

Harriet followed Robert into the kitchen. The smells, the hustle and the bustle were all so familiar. They hurried through the building. He opened door after door. Row after row of hospital beds filled each room. Harriet couldn't believe what she was seeing. Some men were lying down with bandaged heads and arms. One soldier was sitting in a wheelchair with a stump where his leg should be. There were men with thick cotton bandages covering both eyes. Nurses busied themselves, making beds, checking charts and talking to the injured soldiers.

When they opened the door to one room a nurse approached them.

"Can I help you?" she asked.

Harriet froze, unable to speak.

"We're looking for the kitchens," Robert said.

"Well, they're not here. Go back down this hall, and you'll find someone to help."

Robert's quick thinking impressed Harriet. He was a convincing liar. The nurse watched as they walked back the way they'd come, but as soon as the nurse closed the door, Robert turned and ran for the stairs.

As they climbed to the second floor, Harriet asked her cousin, "Why are you helping me?"

"I have my reasons. Do you know this floor is haunted?"

"There is no such thing as ghosts."

"Tell that to the people who've seen the man in the bowler hat and the girl in the white nightdress."

Harriet felt relieved the conversation had changed, even if she didn't believe Robert. Room after room was full of soldiers lying in bed or sitting around with bandaged parts of their bodies. The war seemed very real, looking at all these wounded men. Harriet wondered if her father was lying in a hospital somewhere, or worse. She pictured a battleship getting bombed and sinking to the bottom of the sea. A lump came to her throat as she opened another door.

In the middle of an almost empty room lay Harriet's mother with Dr. Smith by her side. He listened to her chest with a stethoscope. Her eyes were closed, and her head lay unresponsive on the white pillow. Auntie Helen was sitting on a wooden chair by the bed. Her eyes were red and her face pale.

"If this hospital had an x-ray machine, I'd be able to diagnose with more accuracy," Dr. Smith said. "But unless the army increases my budget, I'll have to keep trying different medicines and hope we find the right one before it's too late."

Harriet let out a tiny gasp, not quite a word, not quite a cry. The adults turned to look at her.

"Harriet, what are you doing here?" Auntie Helen asked.

"You need to leave," Dr. Smith said. "You can come at visiting time, when your mother has rested."

"Go home," Auntie Helen said. "I'll be back soon."

Harriet's aunt got up, walked across the room, turned Harriet's body around and pushed her through the door. The heavy dark wood door closed behind her. Robert stepped out of the shadows.

"Where did you go?" Harriet asked.

"I was here."

"Out of sight."

"No point getting caught, if you can avoid it," Robert said.

Harriet gulped down her tears. She wanted to scream and

stamp her foot. Instead, she ran down the hallway, desperate for fresh air and a way to escape from the suffocating smells of wood polish and disinfectant.

"I helped you find your mother, didn't I?" Robert shouted after her.

She stopped and spun to face him. "Yes, you showed me where she's dying."

"I wasn't given that much. When they took my father to hospital, they promised me I could visit him when he was feeling better. But I never saw him again. Next thing I knew he was dead, and I was being shipped to this awful place."

"I hate you, Robert Edward Davis."

"You're not so great yourself and I'm stuck with you forever."

Harriet burst through the hospital door and charged down the gravel driveway. She'd not get used to living with Robert. He'd done this on purpose, to hurt her, and she'd show him. She'd run away, live on her own, sneak into the hospital to see her mother whenever she wanted and never see Robert again.

Harriet ran straight past Annie's house and into the Davis' house. She grabbed her leather satchel. Her father's picture and letter went in first. Next were her notebook and pencil. She had a review to write. She'd become a famous reporter. Then Robert would treat her well. Next she pushed in a cardigan, clean socks and underwear. Her hand touched her London gas mask in its tin box. She wondered if she should take it with her. People talked about the Japanese attacking Canada. After seeing all those injured soldiers, the war seemed close. Harriet had to survive. She'd show Robert she wasn't stuck in this house. She placed the leather strap of the gas mask over her head and continued to pack.

Her hand reached out to Robert's scout book. She picked up the book and flipped through the pages. There were chapters on how to build a shelter, how to find food, how to build a fire, and what to do if a bear attacks you. She shoved it into her bag next to the photo frame. Guilt threatened to bubble in her brain, but Harriet told herself that Robert owed her.

Next, she went to the kitchen, put her hand in the bread bin and took out a loaf. She added two apples and a lump of cheese, buckled up her satchel and left through the back door, determined never to return.

# CHAPTER NINE
## ALONE

Harriet walked along the road until she reached the path leading to the lake. The trees seemed to call her. Their shade was cool and inviting. Everything looked peaceful, so she half walked, and half scrambled into the forest. Stones rolled away from the trail, and Harriet felt her troubles sliding away with them. When she reached the bottom, she stopped and listened.

At first, all she could hear was her own breathing and the sound of her heart pounding in her chest. She thought about the wild animals that attacked children if they were alone in the forest, then shook her head. She was being silly. Robert's stories were a bunch of lies. The sasquatch wasn't a wild animal about to tear her limb from limb. As for the bears and cougars, Harriet decided to find a place to sit and read the scout book. She'd show Robert she could live on her own.

After a while, the path divided in two. One trail led to Loughlin Lake. So much had happened since her afternoon of sunshine and games. It was hard to think of it as the same universe, let alone the same day. Her mother lay in the hospital and Robert thought he could boss her around forever. He was wrong. She didn't need him or his family.

Somewhere nearby, water trickled in a stream. She'd need

water to survive. If she walked to the lake, someone would see her and take her home. She turned towards the babbling water and walked into the unknown.

It wasn't long before she came across a rocky stream. The shallow water was flowing over smooth rocks. Harriet took off her shoes and socks and waded in. She felt the stream push against her ankles. Harriet cupped her hands and splashed her face with the cool, clear water. Taking a bath would be impossible; the water was too cold and shallow.

"Oh well," Harriet said. "I can please myself. I never have to bathe again."

She sniffed the air. Something smelled awful, and it wasn't her. Maybe animals didn't wash. She felt as if someone was watching her. She froze, forcing herself to look out into the forest. Nothing was there, but it was hard to see more than a few trees deep.

"I'll be fine," Harriet said to herself. "No need to be scared. I'll be the Wild Child of the Woods. I'll smell so bad no one will ever want me in their house again."

Harriet took out her braids and shook her long hair.

On the far side of the stream, a curious squirrel scurried down a tree trunk, picked up something in its front paws and ate. Harriet remembered something she'd learned in Sunday School:

"Look at the birds in the air; they do not sow or store away in barns, and yet their Heavenly Father feeds them. Are you not much more valuable than they?"

"Yes, I am valuable. I'll eat from the forest, drink from the stream. All I need is food and shelter before it gets dark."

Harriet waded out of the water and dried her feet on some leaves. She sat on a rock by her backpack, put on her shoes and socks, and took out the bread. She ripped off a chunk and took an enormous mouthful. No table manners here. She copied the squirrel, held the bread to her mouth with two hands, nibbled and looked around.

Harriet threw a small piece of crust at the squirrel. It moved closer to her. Harriet saw some dried blood on its ear.

"Nutty? You poor thing. I'll look after you."

She took a step towards the animal and threw it another crumb. One step, pause, another, pause. Harriet concentrated on getting close to the squirrel.

Crack. A stick broke under someone's feet. The squirrel scampered off into a tree. Harriet looked up. The forest was still, birds had stopped singing, the wind and Harriet's breathing froze. Only the sound of running water, mingled with the beat of Harriet's racing heart, filled the silence.

"Hello? Is anyone there?"

Nothing. Harriet wanted to run away, but she refused to allow fear to defeat her new-found freedom. She took a deep breath and locked her fear away. Until she understood the forest, she'd pretend everything was okay in her new home.

"Well, whoever you are, you need a bath. You're as smelly as the hairy giant I saw this afternoon. And if you're that dirty, you probably need food as well."

Harriet tore off a piece of bread and tossed it to the stink. The bread landed on the ground and sat there.

There was a long pause.

"I can't waste food. If you won't eat it, I won't give you any more."

A raindrop hit Harriet's head. She looked up through the branches and felt another drop land on her face. She had to find shelter soon. Her gaze returned to the place she had thrown the bread. It was gone, but the smell was as strong as ever. She ripped a second, bigger piece of bread off the loaf and tossed it to the ground.

"Hey, I need to get out of the rain. Whoever, or whatever you are, can you help me?"

Long hairy fingers emerged from behind a huge Douglas fir. Harriet stared as an arm stretched towards the bread. A lump formed in Harriet's throat—a scream wanted to erupt but

Harriet swallowed it down. Then a face appeared, ape-like with large inquisitive eyes, heavy eyebrows and a flat forehead.

Harriet forced a smile. Her voice shook as she spoke.

"Hello," Harriet said. "You must be Bigfoot, the sasquatch I saw earlier. You don't seem so scary."

The creature grunted and lifted the bread to its mouth.

Harriet held out her hand and felt raindrops falling.

"Can you help me?"

The creature tilted its head and considered Harriet.

"I have more food here." Harriet reached for her bag. The giant beast turned and walked away.

"Wait. Please. I have to find shelter."

The sasquatch paused, looked over its broad, powerful shoulders and gestured to Harriet. She took a step forward and placed her shoe in the giant's footprint. The creature turned and lumbered into the forest with its arms swinging down near its knees.

"Hey, not so fast," Harriet called.

The rain fell heavily. Harriet could feel it through her cotton blouse. It wouldn't be long before she was soaked through. She shivered and ran to catch up. There were times Harriet could see her new friend and moments when all she had were muddy footprints among the roots and undergrowth.

"Where are you taking me? I need to get undercover."

Their path was taking them up, somewhere into the mountains, maybe to the creature's home, somewhere in the forests around Loughlin. The rain kept falling, and each tree looked like the next. Stories of Little Red Riding Hood and Hansel and Gretel jumped into Harriet's mind. Nothing good came from following paths into the woods.

She wished she could see the stars. Then she'd try to remember her father's lessons about constellations. If he were here, he'd know where they were. If he were here, they'd build a shelter, wait for the rain to pass and navigate their way home. If he were here, she wouldn't be out in the forest at night being led by an animal that may want to eat her.

"Daddy, this is all your fault," Harriet cried. "None of this would happen if you hadn't gone to war and sent me away to this horrid place."

Harriet's legs ached. Her body was wet and cold. She couldn't give up, even if she wanted to. Harriet didn't know where she was. She should've marked the path as she'd walked— breadcrumbs or broken twigs would've worked. She looked back. The rain was washing out her footprints. She was lost and still the creature kept walking.

Finally, they came across a dirt road. Harriet guessed it was a logging track. They stepped onto it and continued uphill. Harriet knew the town was at lake level, far below where they were. Downhill must lead back to the bakery, the Davis' house, her cousins and the hospital. Harriet's confidence grew as she figured out where she was, and a plan formulated in her mind. She knew most of the loggers had left to fight the Nazis. If she could find one of the logger's cabins, she could live in it, visit her mother and wait out the war.

Harriet's clothes were soaking, but she imagined lighting a fire in the hearth, finding a jar of abandoned jam or pickles and a bed with scratchy blankets. Her footsteps and heart lightened, and the gap closed between her and her guide.

"Hey, do you ever talk?" Harriet asked. "My name's Harriet. Thank you for helping me."

Without warning, the creature spun around. Grabbed Harriet and rolled into the undergrowth at the side of the road. She felt a tough leathery hand cover her mouth, deadening any noise Harriet tried to make. She wriggled and kicked the creature. It was no good. The embrace held her prisoner. The creature's wet fur felt rougher than Harriet expected, and the smell was overpowering. Perhaps she should play dead. Harriet had read somewhere that was a good way to escape a wild animal. She forced her body to calm down as her mind analyzed the situation. The creature wasn't hurting her. It seemed alert, listening. Then Harriet heard it too. There came the rumbling of an engine, closely followed by headlights coming up the road.

Harriet watched as an ambulance sped past them, spraying muddy water from the puddles on the road. There was no siren. It seemed oddly out of place for an ambulance to be here, in the middle of nowhere.

Harriet stood slowly once the sound of the engine passed them. The sasquatch didn't stop her. Harriet climbed back onto the road and looked in the direction the ambulance had gone. The sasquatch nodded, and Harriet started following the muddy tire tracks.

When she looked over her shoulder, Harriet realized she was on her own. Her companion had led her to this place and then left her. Harriet felt confused.

She walked along the road imagining a gang of thieves hiding from the police, a famous gangster lying low or spies plotting the invasion of Canada. This would be her scoop. It'd be way more exciting than a movie review.

She came to a clearing. The ambulance stood outside a tiny log cabin.

"Mr. Gunner," she said to herself. "Stop the press. This is going to be an incredible story."

# CHAPTER TEN
## TESTING

Harriet's brain raced. Her wet clothes and grumbling stomach didn't bother her as she walked towards the cabin. An instinct, a warning in her head, told her not to go to the door. Instead, she moved off the road, hid behind a tree and listened. She heard the dripping of rain on the soft ground. Her body shuddered. She should've brought a raincoat.

Harriet heard the cabin door and pressed herself against the trunk of a tree. Footsteps echoed over the wooden patio, down the steps and across the muddy road. The ambulance door opened. Harriet peeked from her hiding place.

"This one's heavy," one man complained.

"Shut it," a second voice replied.

"I'm not doing this again," the first voice said.

A light flickered from the cabin.

One man stooped and placed his end of a stretcher on the ground. A blanket covered someone.

"They're murderers!" Harriet thought.

She pressed her body into the rough bark and listened.

"You'll do it when you're told to," a third voice said. "Get this patient inside before pneumonia sets in."

Harriet knew the voice.

"You can't order me around."

"Then leave."

Harriet could see the men holding their ground like a standoff in a Western.

"But don't expect payment."

"The sheriff should know about these little experiments."

"Are you threatening me? Remember, the sheriff would also like to know how you failed your military medical. You're fit to fight. You're just a coward."

Harriet desperately tried to place the voices. The man in charge sounded so familiar. If Harriet could get a glimpse of his face, she'd know whom to report to the police. She tried to shift her body, but mud squelched underfoot. She had to stay still if she was to go undetected.

"You signed the paper."

"But not with my name. Who are they going to believe—a lying orderly or a respected doctor? Now, get this patient inside. If I can cure lung damage, no one will care where the tests were done."

Dr. Smith! That's who it was. It was her mother's doctor, out here, in the middle of the night, conducting experiments. Harriet wondered whom he'd roped in as assistants.

The men carried the stretcher into the cabin, and the door closed. Harriet's heart thumped in her chest. What tests? Who was on the stretcher? Harriet reached into her bag and pulled out her notebook and pencil. This would be an amazing story for the newspaper.

Rain dripped onto the page, making it impossible to write. Before she became a journalist, she'd have to invent waterproof paper. Should she run to town? She shifted. She wasn't sure if she knew the way. And it was possible no one would believe her. They might think she was making it all up. She had to know more.

Slowly, Harriet crept to the building. There was a window in the back. Harriet held the window ledge and stretched on tiptoes. In the flickering light of a lantern she could see hooks on the log beams, hung with ropes, metal traps, saws and axes. It looked like the ceiling in Herr Schmidt's general store. Jars and books covered the shelves on the walls.

Harriet saw a hand reach up and take something from the shelf. If she was taller, she'd be able to see whom the hand belonged to. Some logs were set up in a circle a short distance from the cabin. Perhaps the loggers used to sit there and rest, eat their lunch and drink coffee together. Harriet pushed a log onto its side and rolled it across the muddy ground.

She stepped onto the log and stared through the window. The doctor's back was towards her. He was mixing something in a mortar and pestle, making notes as he worked. Someone lay on the bed, asleep. One man was arranging wood in the fireplace. Harriet moved her body to see where the second stretcher-bearer was. As she did so, the log shifted under her, throwing her off balance. The log wobbled, and she fell with a thud.

"Someone's out there."

Harriet heard heavy footsteps scramble across the cabin and burst out of the door. She picked herself up and ran into the forest. The undergrowth was thick and wet. Low branches scratched her bare legs. She tripped on roots, scraping her elbow and knee. Harriet crawled into some bushes and found a hollowed tree stump. She climbed inside and pressed her face against a hole in the bark. A flashlight beam hit the stump, momentarily blinding Harriet. She held her breath.

"There's nothing here," the first man said.

"There was someone at the window," the second man said.

"And how did that 'someone' get out here? On a night like this? No one knows we're here, and that's the way it has to remain."

"I heard something."

"You've been spooked by too many old ghost stories. It was probably a bear and we're out here without a gun. I'm going in before I become someone's dinner."

Harriet watched as the flashlight turned away from her. She didn't move until she heard the cabin door close in the distance.

Harriet scrambled out of the log, sat in the rain and thought about what she'd seen. No amount of teasing and cousin noise was as bad as this. She had to tell someone, but how? If she followed the road to town, she would be out in the open and may get caught by the men returning in the ambulance. If she stayed where she was until the ambulance left, she would get attacked by wild animals. If she tried to find another way out of the forest, without her guide, she'd fall down a cliff or be lost forever.

Her knee stung, and Harriet felt warm liquid dripping to her socks. She wiped what she hoped was rain, but found something thick and sticky on her fingers. She raised her hand to her mouth. The sweet, metallic taste of blood brought tears to her eyes. "Why did I run away?" She didn't even know how to find her way back and did not know whom they had in the cabin. Harriet couldn't even write what she had seen.

Tears flowed freely as she wandered through the forest. She felt more alone than ever.

In a voice that wasn't quite a prayer, wasn't quite a whisper, Harriet cried, "Help."

Slowly, she noticed a presence, a warmth beside her. She turned and fell into the outstretched arms of her friend, the sasquatch.

# CHAPTER ELEVEN
## BREAKFAST

When Harriet opened her eyes, sun streamed through the trees and mist rose from the wet forest floor. She lay on a soft, mossy bed under a rocky outcrop. It was not quite a cave but had kept the rain off. She had a blanket of woven leaves and bark over her body. Bird song had replaced the night noises.

She wondered when she'd fallen asleep. The last thing she remembered was the warm, comfortable and safe feeling of having Bigfoot's arms wrapped around her, listening to the terrifying night noises—owls hooting, wolves howling and the constant scritch-scratch of claws hunting for food. It was like her father's embrace when she'd had a nightmare or run to him during a thunderstorm. Now, a woodpecker hammered away at a tree trunk, finches sung to each other and a crow squawked an ugly alarm call. Don't crows gather around dead flesh? Harriet sat bolt upright to show the world she was very much alive. Her body was stiff and sore. She pushed the cover off and looked at her grazed and bruised legs. Her finger traced the edge of a scab forming on her knee.

A grunt startled Harriet, and she looked up to see the sasquatch coming from the mist. Harriet shifted backward to the wall of her shelter. Something about this gigantic creature, her rescuer, made her feel nervous, uncertain. Its powerful frame made Harriet talk nervously. She wanted to find the answers to the questions whizzing through her brain—where was this creature's family, were they alone in the forest, had they both run away, could they be friends? Maybe this was the story Mr. Gunner asked her to find.

The creature took a step towards Harriet and placed a bark platter on the ground. On it, there were berries, strips of raw fish and plant shoots covered in soft creamy-green hairs. Harriet suddenly noticed how hungry she felt. She reached out her hand, then remembered Robert's warning about not coming between a wild animal and its food. Her hand hovered until the sasquatch pushed the plate a little closer to her. Harriet took a fistful of berries and stuffed them into her mouth. The beast did the same. The hairy fingers held out a piece of raw fish. Harriet knew you had to cook chicken and pork all the way through to avoid being poisoned. Was that true of fish? The creature grunted and thrust the fish closer to Harriet's face. She took the offering and raised it slowly to her mouth. It smelled good. Fresh. She placed it between her lips and took a nibble. It tasted good, like the rich smell of the forest after the storm of the night before. Harriet imagined the fish muscles binding with her own, giving her strength, making her as strong as her new friend. She ate strip after strip of the pink flesh, copying her companion picking the bones out of her mouth before swallowing. The last treat was the plant shoots. Harriet watched the creature hold a plant shoot in its long fingers. It scraped a nail along the outside, peeled back the hairy outer skin of the plant, and crunched down on the whitish flesh. Harriet copied. If the plant didn't poison Bigfoot, she'd be okay. This creature didn't wear clothes and hadn't spoken to her but seemed more human than wild animal, like the ancient ape-men she'd seen in an encyclopaedia.

"Thanks," Harriet said.

The sasquatch continued to peel the juicy shoots and chew them between enormous molars.

"We have to eat with our mouth closed," Harriet said.

She showed chewing with her mouth open, then closed her lips together and continued to eat. The sasquatch mirrored Harriet and it's facial muscles became distorted with effort. Suddenly, the creature let out a sound somewhere between a choke and a laugh. Fibrous strands of plant shot across the bark platter and landed in Harriet's hair.

"Ah, that's disgusting!" Harriet shouted, but found the surprise quickly dissolved into laughter.

The creature bent over, picked out food from Harriet's hair and put it back into its mouth. They continued to eat in silence, observing each other, imitating movements—a tilt of the head, a twinkle in the eye, a smile. Harriet noticed how comfortable she was with the silence. She had food, shelter and company. She was happy. The events of the night before felt like a nightmare. The way the men spoke, the fear of being found, the chase through the forest, the fall, seemed like a dream. For all she knew, it was one of her stories. She no longer knew what was real and what was in her imagination. She leaned forward and touched the sasquatch. The animal reacted as if it had received an electric shock. It pulled its long arm away and turned to leave.

"Don't go. Don't leave me. Please. I wanted to check you weren't a dream."

The creature looked over its shoulder, walked away, stopped by a trickle of water, held out its open palms and drank long slow gulps. Harriet stood up. She followed the sasquatch and drank from the clean mountain water.

"My name's Harriet."

The creature stared at her.

"Harr-i-et."

"Ah-ee-e."

Harriet wanted to jump up and down. She felt excitement buzz around her body at the sound of her name.

"Yes, Harriet. My name's Harriet. What's your name?"

There was another tilt of the creature's head.

Placing a hand on her chest, Harriet repeated her name. Then, being careful not to touch her new friend, Harriet held out her hand and repeated her question, "What's your name?"

"Oo-ahn."

"Oo-ahn?" Harriet copied. "Oo-ahn, like Susan."

The creature nodded its head and hit its chest with an open palm. Saying over and over again, "Oo-ahn, oo-ahn, oo-ahn."

"You're a girl?"

Harriet resisted the temptation to look away from her new friend's face, and search for signs of gender. Her friend's body was muscular and covered in long hair. There was no evidence of breasts. She thought of her own body with its flat chest. Perhaps Susan was young, not quite a woman yet.

Harriet looked into the creature's kind eyes. She thought about the embrace the night before when she was cold and scared. It didn't feel like a child's hug. It was more like the feeling she got when she used to run into her father's study. He would look up from his reading, place his pipe in the ashtray, take her up in his arms and swing her off her feet.

"So princess," her father used to say. "What adventure shall we go on today?"

Then he'd walk to the globe. "Shall we sail around Cape Horn?" He'd swing Harriet in his arms, making wild storm noises as if their ship was being tossed close to rocks. "Shall we take a plane to the arctic?" He'd then run around the study imitating engine noises until he came to a stop, stepped out of the imaginary plane and shivered until Harriet giggled uncontrollably. "Or shall we ride kangaroos across the Australian desert?" As Harriet's dad jumped up and down, Harriet would squeal with delight until her mother came in to discover what the noise was all about. They'd end up having tea and biscuits in a tent made from a sheet weighted on the table with the desk lamp and draped over chairs.

Harriet thought of her dad, fighting on the sea, and her

mother struggling for every breath. She wished she could turn back the clock, live in a simpler time with imaginary adventures and friends who would do what she told them to do. Here she had run away—from her cousins, from the men in the cabin— but her life had caught up with her. Harriet was afraid. Afraid her father would be killed in battle, her mother would die in hospital and she'd be alone. A lump formed in her throat. Tears forced their way into her eyes.

Susan Sasquatch leaned in and wiped a tear from Harriet's cheek. Human and beast touched hands. Harriet grabbed Susan's hairy arm with a sudden, desperate realization. It replaced her fear. She'd never be alone if she became famous, and here was her chance.

Everyone would want to know the brilliant reporter who exposed the doctor and proved Bigfoot's existence in one perfect article. All she needed was to gather evidence with Robert's Box Brownie camera.

"I have to go back," Harriet said.

# CHAPTER TWELVE
## STANDOFF

Susan hugged Harriet and took her by the hand. They walked side by side through the forest. Harriet whimpered softly. Her knee and elbow stung. She tried to distract herself by writing the night's events in her head, but every way she spun the words together, they sounded like the tales she made up to get out of trouble.

"Girl Rescued by Sasquatch."

"Secret Laboratory Discovered in the Forest."

"Doctor Arrested."

"Brilliant Young Journalist Exposes Evil Experiments."

No one would believe her. She needed evidence, photos or an eyewitness report, and she needed them now! Harriet picked up her pace, determined to get home—resolve growing with each painful step.

Harriet's impatience grew when Susan stopped by a stream. Beside the rushing water, there were several still, dark pools with steaming water. Susan climbed in, slowly at first, then sinking in like it was a bath. The sasquatch beckoned to Harriet.

"I don't have time," Harriet said. "I have to get back."

Harriet's new friend was insistent, stubborn even. Is this how Bee felt when Harriet pushed her to do things she didn't want to do? Thoughts screamed inside Harriet's head. She didn't have time to soak in a hot spring pool, but saying no to this new friend seemed impossible.

Harriet slipped off her shoes and socks. Took off her pinafore dress, button-up blouse and touched her toe to the water. She quickly withdrew it. The water was hotter than any bath she'd experienced. Susan let out a throaty guffaw and held out her hand. Harriet descended slowly. First her toes, then feet, knees, thighs until her entire body—underwear and all—slipped into the pool. The warm water felt so good. Troubles melted away with the dirt and grime. Harriet's thoughts slowed down.

"This is good," Harriet said. "But I have to go."

Harriet tried to get out of the hot spring, but Susan placed a hand on her shoulder. They sat in silence for a long time. She looked her companion in the eye and wondered if Susan would ever let her go. Harriet had heard about POWs—Prisoners of War. Harriet had no way of knowing what Susan intended. She didn't feel like a prisoner, but she didn't feel free either. Here in the forest, there were no uniforms, weapons or radio broadcasts announcing who the enemy was and what they were doing. Harriet only had her mind and instinct to give her information. They told her she was safe, being cared for and was being prepared for what she had to face. In the silence, Harriet's strength and courage grew. She took a deep breath and allowed plans to formulate in her mind.

After some time and without words, the two rose. A ray of sunlight came through the trees, warm and enlightening. Harriet sat on a smooth rock. Steam rose from her body and joined the mist rising between the trees. Harriet watched Susan walk around picking plants and placing them in her mouth. The sasquatch chewed and chewed then spat a fibrous clump out into her hand, felt the gooey mush and returned it to her enormous molars. She picked more plants and added them to her mouth. Finally, Susan approached Harriet, spat the clump into her hand and placed it on Harriet's grazed knee and elbow.

"Ewww! That's disgusting."

Susan held the mulch against Harriet's grazes. The burning pain eased. Harriet felt whole again. It was incredible, a miracle. Maybe this is what the doctor was looking for—plants with the power to heal. Imagine getting this to injured soldiers. She had a miracle cure to add to her story. She would be famous, extraordinary. Harriet ran her fingers over the Sasquatch's soft fur covering its head and lifted Susan's chin, so their eyes met.

"Thank you. I need to go now, but I'll come back."

Harriet got up, reached into her satchel, took out clean, dry underwear and got dressed. She realized she didn't know where she was.

"I need to go home."

Susan Sasquatch got up and walked away. Harriet froze. Her friend was leaving.

"Please, don't leave me alone. I need your help."

Susan looked over her broad shoulders and beckoned to Harriet. Then the Sasquatch led the way through the forest. Harriet hoped she was on her way to Loughlin and not her new forest home.

Harriet's legs ached. The sun climbed higher and higher until the shafts of light came from directly above the forest. If only she had a map and a compass.

Of course, that was the way she'd make people believe her. She'd go to the library, find a map and gather evidence. She'd present it like the lawyer in *The Trial*. He'd made the whole courtroom believe a child knew the truth. She wouldn't tell anyone about the cabin in the forest until she had evidence.

Excitement rose in Harriet's body and with it came annoyance. She had to get her plan underway instead of following a lumbering giant through the forest. Once again, Susan paused.

"Why are you stopping?"

Susan didn't answer. She never answered. She continued in her own way, waded into the stream they'd been following and squatted on a rock. Her long arms swung over the surface of the running water. Frustration rose from the pit of Harriet's stomach. She wanted to keep going but didn't know where she was. When she returned to the forest, she'd make sure she didn't need any help. She'd be better off on her own.

Harriet's thoughts were broken when a fish jumped out of the water. Susan's hands moved at lightning speed and caught a salmon mid-flight. She lifted the wriggling fish to her mouth and bit down on its neck. The flapping stopped and Susan ripped flesh, placed one piece in her mouth and gave another to Harriet. They ate the raw pink flesh together. It tasted good, and Harriet felt strength return to her mind and body. Harriet rinsed her hands in the fast-running water, cupped her hands together and took long, cold, clear gulps of water. Harriet hated to admit it, but she'd needed the food.

"Can we go now? Please."

Harriet looked at her friend. Susan's body was like a statue. The sasquatch's attention was focused upstream. Harriet followed her gaze. A bear stared at Susan. The two animals fixed their eyes on each other. Harriet backed away to the safety of a tree. In unison, Susan and the bear rose onto their back legs and drew their bodies to full height. They let out deafening roars. The bear's front paws landed in the water and the powerful creature took two giant strides towards Susan. They were going to fight each other. Over what? Salmon? Territory? Susan stood her ground. The bear came to a halt, bared her teeth, barked at Susan, turned and lumbered off. The sasquatch watched until the bear was out of sight. Then her body relaxed, and she turned away from the stream.

Harriet ran from her hiding place and hugged her friend. Susan grunted and pushed Harriet onto a path leading down the mountain. Something had changed. There were no more food breaks, no fingers run through Harriet's hair and no smiles. Instead of leading the way, Susan pushed Harriet ahead of her along the descending path. The gaps between nudges got longer and Harriet noticed Susan was hanging back. Harriet felt like she was in trouble. She'd caused a problem but didn't know how or why.

When Harriet stopped getting poked in the back, she turned to find she was on her own. Her body trembled. Images of a bear attack sprang to mind. Harriet tightened her muscles and refused to acknowledge her nervousness.

"Leave me. See if I care. I can look after myself. I don't need you. I don't need anyone."

Harriet continued along the path. Instinctively, she jumped at every rustle in the trees. Bird song startled her. Every step made being alone more difficult. Harriet took a deep breath. She couldn't smell her sasquatch friend anymore. The earthy pine scent was so different to home. Harriet thought about her mother's perfume and her father's pipe. A tear formed in the corner of her eye. Her stomach growled. Harriet picked some salmon berries and longed for fresh bread, butter and jam.

Harriet tried to focus her mind on gathering evidence, but her thoughts kept drifting. She was told the Davis' place was now home, but Harriet didn't want to belong there. She was told England was no longer safe—the Germans were bombing London. Here, everything had gone wrong. Harriet didn't know where her father was or whether he was even alive. Her mother was sicker than ever, and the doctor did secret tests in a cabin in the forest. Her only friend, a creature people didn't believe existed, had left her. Harriet felt a tear roll down her face. She tried to wipe it away, but more tears flowed, and Harriet slumped down onto a rock. She needed time to think. Her brain was a swirling mass with thoughts disappearing into a tornado.

"Harriet!"

Robert stood in front of her. Harriet rubbed her eyes in disbelief.

"Half the town is out looking for you. Where have you been?"

Harriet watched Robert take something from his pocket and lift it to his mouth.

"Wait," Harriet said. "I've seen some things out here. Don't let anyone know you've found me. I just need your camera and one more day."

Their eyes met. Robert blew hard on a whistle. The loud, piercing noise scattered birds into the air.

"She's over here! I've found her!"

Harriet turned and ran away from her cousin. He lunged forward and grabbed her arm.

"Let me go! You don't understand. You don't know what's out here."

"You're out here! And you shouldn't be."

Harriet stomped her foot and tried to yank her arm from Robert's grasp. "I'm not going back!"

"You're killing your mother."

In a split second of guilt, Harriet softened. She needed to know whether her mother had survived the night, and in that moment, Robert tackled Harriet to the ground.

"Get off me!"

"No! You're coming home and staying home!"

Harriet struggled, but she was no match for her cousin once he'd pinned her arms to the ground above her head.

Then, from the forest, came an earth-shattering roar. Harriet and Robert jerked their heads in the direction of the noise. They saw Susan Sasquatch's teeth and the dark tunnel of her throat.

Harriet froze. Susan stepped forward. For a moment, children and sasquatch stared at each other. Susan's back hunched over, her brow furrowed, and fur bristled like porcupine needles. Robert scrambled off Harriet. He tried to blow on the whistle, but no sound came. Harriet remained rooted to the spot.

With a bellow, the sasquatch ran towards Robert. She came faster than Harriet would have believed possible. Susan galloped through the trees, her muscles heaving. Before Robert could even raise his arms to protect himself, Susan was right in front of him.

And then, just inches away from Robert, Susan planted her

arms and slid to a stop. Pine needles and mud piled up in front of the sasquatch's hands. Harriet froze—too petrified to look away, too terrified to watch. She trembled as Susan gnashed her teeth at Robert.

If Susan was going to kill Robert, there was nothing Harriet could do. She couldn't fight this wild force of nature, this creature who'd brought her breakfast, tended her wounds, shown her the path home—her friend. Harriet felt like screaming, but she couldn't even do that. She felt so small, so helpless, so weak.

"Please don't kill him," Harriet whispered.

Susan roared and bared her teeth. Robert staggered to his feet, tried to back away, and slipped on a mossy rock. He thumped down on the forest floor and squirmed backward.

Step by step Susan Sasquatch came closer until her hand grabbed Robert's foot. She sniffed at Robert's sock, his pants and his buttoned shirt. Harriet could see the twitching nostrils of a wild animal. She could hear its breath going in and out. Robert stopped moving. Susan straddled Robert with her long legs. She sniffed at his chest. Harriet had seen nothing so big and frightening. Her friend was enormous. Sinewy muscles covered the sasquatch's legs, thick hairs stood on her back and angry snorts erupted from her flaring nostrils. Harriet stared as Susan's nose touched Robert's chin. Sasquatch lips brushed his neck. Robert was breathing in the air that Susan breathed out. As this wild animal sniffed, Robert cried.

"Please don't," Harriet said again.

Susan raised her head and stood to her full height. Maybe she understood Harriet's words, maybe not. It didn't matter. Susan had made it very clear who owned the forest, whose territory Harriet and Robert were in. She had stood her ground and established dominance. Robert had to leave, like the bear had done earlier.

Harriet looked from Robert to her new friend. She realized the horror of the attack had been an attempt to defend her. Susan had seen Robert as the enemy. Robert lay, small and weak with dirty tear streaks on his cheeks. Harriet had pleaded for his safety. They were connected now. Humans invading another world. Susan had used all her strength to show who was boss, and Harriet had defended her cousin. She had chosen her side. Terror gripped her heart. Going home with Robert meant facing her mother, the doctor, and the trouble she'd be in for running away. But living in the forest was no longer the straightforward choice. Susan was so human, caring and protective, yet wild and angry. Harriet and Robert were in Susan's space. Harriet moved slowly until she was close enough to wipe a tear from Robert's face. She took his hand and pulled him to his feet. Susan turned and took a step away.

Then a gunshot shattered the silence.

## CHAPTER THIRTEEN
## SHOT

Harriet, Robert and Susan turned instinctively to the noise. Through the trees, they saw Dr. Smith with his smoking rifle pointing to the sky. Susan bared her teeth as the barrel lowered. The doctor took aim. The sasquatch's eyes narrowed, her nostrils flared, and Harriet saw the dark tunnel of her throat as another roar shook the forest. Susan had a new target for her anger.

"Get down! Get away!" Dr. Smith shouted.

"No! Don't hurt her," Harriet cried.

Harriet leapt to her feet. She dived into the space between the doctor and her ferocious friend. A gunshot exploded. There was a high-pitched ring as metal struck metal, then the bullet burned through her flesh. Harriet tried to land on her feet, but her legs gave way. Before her body hit the forest floor, Susan scooped her up, turned and ran into the forest.

Trees, streams, and shafts of sunlight came and went as Susan carried Harriet deep into the forest. Harriet clenched her jaw and muffled her cries in Susan's fur. She wanted the pain to go away. Each stride sent shock waves drumming through her body. Harriet gulped for air as her gas mask and satchel banged against her side. Her eyes rolled back in her head. She wanted to sleep and forget everything.

Finally, Susan laid Harriet on a soft bank near a steaming pool. Harriet thought about her bath in the hot spring earlier in the day. She wanted to slide into the water and allow the pain to vanish. Susan bent over her and examined the trickle of congealing blood. Susan took Harriet's torn blouse in two hands and ripped it open, exposing the bullet wound.

Harriet gasped, gritted her teeth and waited for her friend to work her healing magic.

Susan took a handful of moss and dipped it into the pool. Slowly and carefully, the sasquatch lowered her hand and cleaned dry blood from Harriet's arm. The warm water felt good, comforting. Harriet allowed her eyes to close, but Susan prodded her awake. The pain in her shoulder made breathing hard. Harriet longed to sob, but her body ached too much for movement. She longed for her brain to calm down and stop asking questions. Why had the doctor, a healer, become the destroyer? Harriet wondered if she'd die here in the forest. She prayed she would see her mother and father again.

Susan Sasquatch busied herself. She collected stinging nettle stalks and flicked them at the wound. Tears poured down Harriet's face until she begged for the torture to stop. Then the warm, soft moss returned to ease the pain. Nettles, moss, nettles, moss. Harriet knew Susan was trying to help her, but it felt more like punishment, torture for being in the wrong place at the wrong time. Eventually, Susan used her long, leathery fingers to pick lead shot from the blood on her arm and shoulder. Somehow, Harriet had rejected these metal fragments and she lay in amazement at her friend's knowledge and understanding.

Next, Susan picked leaves from plants and placed them in her mouth. Harriet watched her friend's jaw move as she chewed the herbs. Eventually, Susan took a small ball of dark green mush from her mouth, rolled it in her palm and pushed the poultice into Harriet's mouth. It tasted bitter. Harriet wanted to spit it out, but the Sasquatch held her jaw shut with one finger pressed gently on the patient's chin. Susan's big, brown eyes made it clear to Harriet that the sticky ball must stay. Instead of fighting the urge to barf at the saliva-herb ball inside her mouth, Harriet relaxed and found her breathing eased.

"Thank you," Harriet said.

Susan turned her attention back to the wounded shoulder. She sniffed it, felt around it and examined it so closely she and Harriet shared the same air. Then Harriet's rescuer got back to work. She ripped up plants, washed roots in the hot spring pool, chewed them and spat them onto some bark. She added leaves to the mix. Then Susan took a smooth rock, the size of her enormous hand, and ground the plant mix into a paste.

Susan brought the medicine to her patient, took up some fresh moss, cleaned out the wound and packed the red, raw flesh with the stringy mess of forest plants. She took Harriet's opposite hand and used it to cover the wound. Harriet tried to lift her hand to look, but Susan put her hand on top of hers. It was clear Harriet was expected to press down on the open flesh and let the healing magic work. For the first time since arriving in Loughlin, maybe the first time in her life, Harriet wanted to follow someone else's instructions.

Harriet relaxed, and her friend brought her fresh water in a hollowed-out piece of wood. The sasquatch lifted Harriet's head from the ground, then her shoulders and back. Susan placed her patient against her round soft belly, which became Harriet's pillow, and lifted the welcome drink to Harriet's lips. Finally, Susan allowed Harriet to drift into a deep sleep.

It was dark when Harriet woke. Her body shivered. The wound on her shoulder burned. Pain shot through her body, and breathing was more difficult than ever. Susan Sasquatch pushed another lump of plant spit into Harriet's mouth. She gagged at the bitter taste. The animal's brow furrowed. Far from waking up better, Harriet felt worse. Susan's long hairy fingers tried to take the herb poultice from the wound. Harriet screamed in pain, a raw sound like a lone wolf crying in the wilderness.

Susan packed a fresh poultice over the congealed blood.

Harriet whimpered and tried to move away from her friend's tender touch. The sasquatch stared at her patient, sniffed the gash left by the gunshot, turned and rinsed her hands in the hot springs.

"Don't leave me. Please. I don't want to die. I want to go home."

Tears flowed down Harriet's face. Susan turned back to face the patient. She grunted, picked Harriet up and carried the weeping patient.

Every step was like reliving when the rifle bullet tore through her skin. Movement sent agonizing pain through Harriet's body. She clung to the long hairs on Susan's broad, strong shoulders and sucked on the plant ball in her mouth.

Gradually, the steady steps rocked Harriet into a half sleep. She was vaguely aware of their climb, up, up, up through the forest. Occasionally, Harriet was aware of her surroundings. Frogs jolted her awake. Their mating call was loud and clear in the darkness. Bats darted between salmon berry patches as they were disturbed from their nighttime feasting. An owl hooted as he prepared to hunt, annoyed by the intrusion. She didn't belong here. She didn't belong anywhere.

Harriet thought about the forest carrying on as usual around her, of the animals asleep in their beds or finding their nocturnal meals. She thought about the doctor. How was he going to explain shooting her? She thought about Robert and what he'd said about her, her mother and the place he said that Harriet ought to be. There was so much she needed to go back for. She sucked the juice out of the plant ball in her mouth and sighed as the soothing liquid slipped down her throat. If she survived this, she'd make things right. She'd tell the world about the doctor, make her mother well again and get on with Robert. Suddenly, she understood her father and the men she'd seen marching to war, determined to fight evil, whatever the personal cost.

Harriet shivered and curled in tighter to Susan's warm fur coat. They'd left the forest behind and climbed a rocky mountain. Patches of snow shined in the moonlight. It may be summer by the lake, but up high an icy wind swirled around the rocky outcrops. Harriet pictured the snow-capped peaks she'd seen in the distance when she played in the Davis' yard. They were a long way from Loughlin, and a time when Harriet jumped rope and reluctantly played war with her cousins.

Darkness surrounded them as they entered a cave. Moonlight was shut out, but still they walked, deeper and deeper into the heart of the mountain. Harriet wondered if she was going to die. Here, with her silent friend. She clung to Susan's back. She could hear a trickle of water. Susan cupped her hands and took long gulps. Some water spilled down Susan's neck and onto Harriet's head. It was ice cold. Harriet shivered, curled into Susan's fur and prayed.

"I'm told there's a God out there who cares about me. If there is, please help me through this so I can make everything right again."

Susan continued to walk, slower now, likely exhausted from their travels. Harriet heard the water go from a trickle to a rushing stream. She looked over Susan's shoulder. She could see the moon and thousands of stars. They were nearing the end of the cave. They stood on the edge of a cliff. There was nowhere else to go. A waterfall gushed over the edge and disappeared into the darkness below.

Susan turned to face the mountain and climbed down the rocky cliff face. It terrified Harriet. Cold air froze in her lungs and her heart pounded in her chest. She clung to Susan's back with her good arm but felt sure she would plummet to her death. Rocks slipped under Susan's feet, and the sound echoed as they bounced from one rocky outcrop to another. The sound of rushing water accompanied the click clack of the falling rock.

Finally, they reached a ledge. Susan inched along it, towards the gushing water. Harriet felt certain it would wash her from Susan's back. As they got closer, she saw a gap between the water and the mountain. Behind the waterfall, they found another cave, and Susan squeezed into the gap.

Inside the cave, Susan found a cedar blanket, placed Harriet on it, and waited. Harriet blinked. Through the blackness, Harriet saw Susan stand and greet two sets of approaching eyes.

# CHAPTER FOURTEEN
## MEDICINE WOMAN

Susan let out a series of grunts and whines. Similar sounds came from the direction of the eyes in the cave. Two more sasquatches walked to Susan. They didn't seem happy. Susan stepped aside and showed where Harriet lay. The creatures shook their heads and gnashed their teeth. Susan whimpered, and Harriet cried. They had come so far.

Susan turned her back on the animals, wrapped Harriet in the rough bark blanket, picked up her limp shivering body and walked back towards the waterfall. A barking sound made her turn. One sasquatch beckoned to Susan. The second animal shook its head disapprovingly. The animals argued among themselves until one pushed the other aside. Harriet thought a fight might break out. Instead, the attacker signaled to Susan, and Harriet was carried through a tunnel, out into moonlight.

Susan placed her patient on the ground in a clearing. Harriet found it hard to focus. Her eyes wanted to close and shut out the pain shooting from her shoulder to her lungs. In a blurry vision, eyes, nostrils and teeth circled around her. Harriet longed for another clump of the plant mix Susan had placed in her mouth, for more cooling herbs to be put on her throbbing shoulder. Instead, Susan howled to the growing crowd.

An enormous sasquatch, taller than Susan and twice as broad, sauntered into Harriet's vision. Susan fell silent. The group parted and this leader—because that's the way they treated him—leaned in to sniff Harriet. He pulled himself to his full height and stared down at Susan. Harriet's friend tried to shrink away, but a wall of ape-like creatures met her.

The leader bared his teeth; fur stood on the back of his neck; his eyes glared at Susan. He roared—a sound so terrifying, Harriet forgot about the pain shooting through her body. Susan sniveled. The sasquatch in charge struck Susan across her face with such force Harriet's friend fell to her knees. She clutched her stinging face. The leader turned his back on Susan, walked away from the clearing and disappeared into the forest. The troop of sasquatches followed. Harriet and Susan were alone again.

Her companion sat, clutching her face. Harriet dragged herself across the clearing, pulled herself up on Susan's arm and gently stroked Susan's matted fur. Harriet could see the pain in her friend's face. The slap hurt her, but the rejection—her own kind turning their backs on the sasquatch—was agonizing. Harriet realized she had to be strong and get Susan to find another way to help her. They had not come this far to give up now. Harriet had to get home and take the miraculous herbs to the hospital.

They sat in the clearing as the day grew brighter. Harriet felt the warmth of the sunshine coming through the trees, but her body shivered. She pulled herself closer to Susan's warm, thick fur. She wanted to breathe easily, to run and skip around the Royal Naval College in London with the clipped lawn beneath her bare feet and not a care in the world. Harriet remembered the thrill of breaking rules with her best friend, running through the officers' dining room, stealing biscuits and racing home. Harriet moved her body closer to Susan's. If only these arms were those of her father's. Harriet thought of the way he used to turn his head when she entered his study, lay down his pipe and stand with open arms. Harriet would run and be swept up in his loving embrace.

"How's my princess today?"

Then he'd spin Harriet around until they'd crossed the room to his globe.

"Where shall we go today?"

"Somewhere pink, somewhere pink!" Harriet replied.

"Ah, the British Empire. Look at all the lands ruled by King George! We could ride elephants in India, go on an African safari or play a didgeridoo in the Australian outback."

Harriet wished life were simple again. Her father was so sure about the world. Here, she'd been shot by a doctor. The same man who was healing her mother, and she wasn't sure it was an accident. Harriet had run into the line of fire. She'd protected Susan. Then Susan had sought help and been rejected. Her own kind had turned their backs and left. Harriet thought about her aunt. The way she'd opened her house, cooked meals and welcomed two extra people. She thought about Robert searching for her. She was not alone, not in the way Susan was. Guilt mixed with pain as Harriet thought about her sasquatch friend. Susan had no one.

Harriet removed the herb ball from her mouth and offered it to Susan. The sasquatch pushed Harriet's hand back to her mouth. Harriet tried again. She lifted her hand to Susan's cheek and stroked the gash. Susan turned her head to look at Harriet. She held Harriet's hand in her own. Their eyes met, and Susan smiled. It wasn't the welcome, sunny smile Harriet saw when they first met. It was a knowing smile, an accepting smile, full of pain and understanding, like the smile her mother gave her when she felt too sick to challenge Harriet's defiance.

Susan held Harriet's hand in hers and stood up.

Harriet stretched her arms out towards her rescuer. "Carry me."

The sasquatch shook her head. Harriet stood, her legs weak

and shaky. If she was going to survive, Harriet had to find strength she didn't know she had.

Every step sent painful shocks through her shoulder. Each stinging blow reminded Harriet she was alive and must return to sort out the mess she'd left. Her mother sick in the hospital, her aunt working herself to the bone, Robert doing everything to make her life miserable, and the doctor experimenting on patients in the forest. If she could survive being shot, she was stronger than she believed.

Her painful steps grew stronger until she matched Susan's pace—no longer the victim but the ailing companion. It wasn't long before they came across another cave, and there in the entrance sat a grey, ancient looking sasquatch. Harriet froze, uncertain about the greeting they'd receive.

Slowly, the old woman—because that's what she looked like —raised her head, smiled and invited the travelers into her cave.

Susan hesitated for a moment. Harriet took her friend's hand and followed the old sasquatch in.

It took time for Harriet's eyes to adjust to the darkness. A fire sent a flickering light around the cave. Plants hung drying from cracks in the ceiling, bark trays full of dried berries sat on ledges with strange-shaped roots beside them. The old sasquatch held out her hand and showed Harriet a red-brown mat sitting on a ridge. Harriet walked towards it and sat as if she was in a doctor's office.

There was no white coat, stethoscope or dry sticks placed on her tongue. No words were spoken. Instead, the old sasquatch came close to Harriet, peeled off the herbs, revealed the gunshot wound and sniffed. She held the herb Band-Aid out towards the light of the fire and studied it carefully. Harriet's shoulder stung. The old sasquatch smiled and made a sound somewhere between a purr and a grunt. Her hand reached for some dried leaves. She put them in her mouth, chewed them to a pulp, rolled the fibrous mash in the palms of her hands and held the dark ball to Harriet's lips. Harriet wondered if Susan learned about the healing power of plants from this animal, healer, medicine woman. Harriet didn't know what label to use, but she took the medicine gratefully. The familiar look and taste eased Harriet's breathing within seconds. She had to get this herb to her mother.

Harriet and Susan watched the old sasquatch walk around her den. She took handfuls of herbs, roots and berries. She placed them on a hollowed-out rock, spat on them, then took a smooth rock in her hand and mashed them together. Each time she lowered the rock onto the mixture, a clanking sound echoed around the cave. Susan watched and imitated the moves.

The old sasquatch moved back to Harriet, rinsed the wound with a clump of wet moss and smeared the new herb medicine on the wounded shoulder. Harriet flinched, expecting it to sting. Instead, the mixture sent a calming vibration to her core. Harriet's heart rate slowed, and the pain melted away.

"Thank you," Harriet whispered.

The old medicine woman put one hand on the back of Harriet's head, the other on her chest, and laid her on the bark matting. She brushed the backs of her fur-covered hands over Harriet's eyes and made it clear that Harriet should rest. Harriet's eyelids were heavy. Without the shooting pain in her shoulder, all Harriet's body wanted was sleep. As she drifted off, Harriet wondered how she could get the leaves to her mother. She had no common language to ask for them. She thought about taking them. It wouldn't be stealing. They were only dried leaves. Surely there were more.

Harriet watched her healer place an arm around Susan. The two sasquatches moved to the entrance of the cave. From where she lay, Harriet could see tears rolling down Susan's face. The two creatures—no longer either animal or human in Harriet's mind—sat, talked, and cried together. Harriet longed to know what they were saying. Longed to sit and talk with her mother like days of old when her mother would knit or sew or mend and Harriet would tell her about the games she'd played, the arguments she'd had and the stories she wanted to write.

Slowly, Harriet inched towards the pile of breath-easy herbs. Finally, her hand was close enough. Harriet reached out, took a handful of the flakey leaves and shoved it into her gas mask box. Then she allowed the healing power of sleep to take over.

Harriet woke to the gentle rocking motion of Susan's footsteps. Mist rose through the trees, making it hard to see more than a few yards in front of them. Harriet didn't know whether she'd slept for a few hours or a few days. She could feel her shoulder with each of Susan's long strides. It hurt, but the burning sensation had eased; her breathing was no longer laboured. She felt strength returning to her body. She felt for her gas mask. The familiar metal box with its leather strap was right there, next to her satchel, slung over her good shoulder. She had to get the herbs to her mother.

Finally, Susan stopped and lay Harriet down. There was sand beneath her body. Harriet sat up and looked out over a lake. The sky was ablaze with colour—red, orange, deep purple.

"Red sky in the morning, shepherd's warning."

Harriet's words met silence. Harriet looked around. Her friend was nowhere in sight.

"Susan! Susan!"

Harriet looked to the forest. There, in the rising fog, hidden in the trees, was her friend. She smiled at Harriet, just like she'd done that first day they'd met at Loughlin Lake.

Harriet felt she was somewhere familiar. She turned back to the lake. She could just make out the fishing boats, moored nearby, and the shape of a sandcastle, almost flattened by a footstep.

No sooner did Harriet know where she was than a voice echoed in the distance.

"Over here! There's someone over here!"

# CHAPTER FIFTEEN
## HOSPITAL

The morning passed like a tornado, with Harriet in the storm's eye. She was whisked to Loughlin Hospital where nurses came and went. They took her temperature, felt for a pulse, looked at Harriet's water glass and asked if she'd peed. Her aunt sat by her bed, smudges of flour still on her bakery overalls. Mr. Gunner arrived and asked if he could print her story. He wanted to know how she'd survived, injured and alone in the forest for two nights. Harriet pieced together the timeline from running away to landing in hospital. She couldn't believe so much had happened in less than forty-eight hours.

"I'll write it for you," Harriet said. "It's an amazing story. You'd better hold the front page."

Finally, Harriet found a moment when she was on her own with her aunt.

"How's Mummy?"

Auntie Helen didn't speak for a long time. When she did, her voice crackled.

"She's a little better now she knows you are safe."

Harriet felt guilty, although she didn't understand why. It wasn't her fault she'd been gone so long. She had to get the medicine to her mother.

"Can I see her?"

"The doctor says you should rest first."

"What about Robert, Mickey and Billy?"

"Robert's at the bakery. Mickey and Billy are with Annie. She hopes you get better soon so you can play together."

Susan had rescued her, shown her how to survive, made sure she reached a healer and got her safely back to her people. She missed her sasquatch friend—her smile, her touch, even her smell. Harriet thought about the old sasquatch in the cave, the family sending Susan on her way, and the amazing herbs they knew about. It was incredible to think about the knowledge these wild creatures had. They knew more than human doctors.

"Ah! How's the little survivor?"

Harriet sat up. The last time she'd hear this voice, a bullet ripped through her shoulder. There stood Dr. Smith. He was smiling with his mouth, but eyes told a different story, one of anger and determination.

"You're famous," he said. "The local radio has just announced your survival. 'Loughlin girl, aged twelve, found alive after two nights in the forest. Reports tell us a bear rescued her.'"

"When can I go?" Harriet asked.

"Harriet! Manners please!" Auntie Helen said.

"I think you should rest here for a couple of days," Dr. Smith said. "We'll monitor this gunshot wound. Make sure there's no infection. Let you rest and recover from your ordeal."

"I wouldn't have a bullet in my shoulder if you hadn't shot me."

"Harriet!" Auntie Helen chastised. "What a thing to say! A bear attacked Robert. The doctor did what he had to. You got in the way."

"Don't worry, delusional patients often accuse their healers of attempting to harm them," the doctor said. "You can see how this young lady needs rest. Give her a couple of days and we'll see her right as rain."

Harriet felt her gut tighten and her eyes narrow. She didn't trust the doctor.

"I want to see my mom. Please."

"In time," the doctor said. "First rest. And Mrs. Davis, you can tell Mrs. Hall that Harriet is in expert hands. I'll be up to see her soon. I just want to examine this little survivor."

The doctor leaned over and pinched Harriet's cheek. Together, they watched Auntie Helen leave the room. They listened as her footsteps faded down the hallway.

"Now, I need you to tell me who treated this shoulder for you," the doctor said.

His sudden change in tone and demeanour frightened Harriet. His steel-grey eyes stared down at her, sending a chill up her back. He set a leather doctor's bag on Harriet's bed, opened it and took out the herb poultice.

"Who made this?" the doctor asked.

Harriet pressed her lips closed tightly. She was determined not to tell the doctor about Susan and her forest healer.

"You will tell me."

"I don't know her name."

"Who? A woman?"

"I don't know."

"What do you mean, you don't know? Was it a woman or not?"

Harriet looked away from the doctor. She thought of Susan and the way her family had dismissed her. The loyalty she'd shown as she took Harriet to the old healer. Susan stood by Harriet and returned her safely to her people.

The doctor grabbed Harriet's injured shoulder with one hand and muffled her scream with the other.

"Listen to me, young lady. This hospital is full of soldiers and their gunshot wounds. Every day, people are wounded in this war. They'll come to me for help. I'll operate, remove bullets, stitch gaping wounds, remove mangled limbs torn to shreds by enemy bombs and pray they'll live long enough to see their families again. But nothing I can do will heal them as quickly as this has worked on you."

Harriet stopped screaming and listened. Her brain tried to understand what the doctor was saying.

She hesitated. This was the man who shot her, who was hurting her now, and took patients to a cabin in the forest. If she told the doctor about Susan, she'd betray a friend, but the medical knowledge might help others. Harriet didn't know what to do.

The doctor released his grip and returned to his bag. He removed a small petri dish like the one Harriet used to grow mold in Science. In it were the remains of the dark herb ball Harriet sucked on to ease her breathing and pain.

"Will you tell me about this?"

The doctor's tone softened as he held the dish to the light. Harriet thought about the herbs in her gas mask tin. She had to check they were still there. She had to get them to her mom. Panic took over her body, starting in the pit of her stomach. Pressure rose like a kettle about to boil.

"We both know the tales of the forest—myths, some call them—but we know there are places and plants with incredible power. I want to discover more before men like your father and uncle die in agony, their bodies unable to mend from the wounds inflicted by tyranny."

Harriet looked from the doctor to the ceiling. In her mind, she debated whether she should tell the doctor about the old sasquatch in the forest. She didn't know how to find the cave again. Perhaps Susan would help if Harriet could explain the war to her. Harriet had seen a sasquatch strike her friend. They must have their own battles, maybe their own wars. If the doctor could find medicine to heal soldiers, surely it was her duty to tell him everything she knew. After all, he knew about the sasquatch. He'd seen Susan standing over Robert. It was strange neither Robert nor the doctor had corrected the reports about Harriet being with bears. It was as if they didn't want to admit what they'd seen with their own eyes.

Harriet was about to speak when the door opened, and a familiar voice made Harriet turn her head.

"Ah! I've found the young lady who survived two nights in the forest with bears."

The doctor greeted Herr. Schmidt, the German shopkeeper. Harriet looked from one man to the other. The doctor's forehead furrowed, and his teeth clenched in annoyance before a fake smile spread across his face.

"With your permission, Doctor, I've brought a gift for your patient," Herr. Schmidt said. "People think Stollen and Christmas go together. But I find it's good for any celebration, and this little girl was the only good piece of news on the radio today. You're quite a celebrity."

Harriet's brain whirred into overdrive. Here stood a German shopkeeper; he'd brought her a gift and appeared friendly. Harriet didn't want to believe anything she'd been told by her cousin, but what if Herr Schmidt was the German spy Robert believed him to be? Harriet looked from one man to the other. They obviously knew each other. Anything she told the doctor could go straight to the enemy. She closed her mouth, determined to keep the secrets of the forest from the doctor and Herr Schmidt.

The shopkeeper opened the parcel and took out an oval-shaped loaf, sprinkled with sugar. Thick slices fell away from the gift as Herr Schmidt offered the treat to Harriet and the doctor. The smell of warm marzipan and candied peel filled the room. Harriet's mouth watered as she took a piece and lifted it to her mouth. She stopped herself from taking a bite as she wondered whether truth serum or poison infused the treat.

Harriet watched the doctor take his slice and place it on the bedside table. He brushed his hands together, took out a notebook and started writing in it. Harriet decided not to eat the Stollen until she'd seen one of these men bite into their slice first.

Harriet lowered the delicious smelling treat away from her mouth.

"Eat up," the shopkeeper said. "It'll give you strength. You'll be skipping back into my store before you know it, cheering up my day with tales of your mischievous cousins."

Harriet panicked. She tried to remember the stories she'd told the storekeeper. A radio slogan played in her head: "Careless talk costs life."

She looked for a way to escape. The doctor had stopped writing. He placed his notebook back into his bag, took out a large needle and a bottle of clear liquid. With the syringe ready, the doctor bent over Harriet, wiped her arm and jabbed it with the needle.

"I must get on," the German said. "I'll just pop my head in to see your mother and let her know that I've seen you with my own eyes."

"Can I come?" Harriet said. "I have to see her."

"Rest first," the doctor said. "We'll talk later about what you can and can't do during your recovery."

The room started to spin and Harriet's eyes closed. She wanted to call for help, tell someone about the doctor working with a German spy. But no words came out of her mouth and she slipped into a deep sleep.

Harriet woke to the noise of her cousins entering the room.

"I want to see it first," Billy said.

"No, show me. Where'd you get shot?" Mickey said.

"You're famous," Billy said. "You're on the radio."

"Did you really stay with a bear?" Billy asked.

"Now then boys, Harriet must rest," Auntie Helen said. "You're being way too boisterous."

"But a bear," Billy repeated. "You stayed with a bear. That's unbelievable."

"Yes, it is," Robert said.

Harriet hadn't noticed her older cousin standing near the door. He stared at Harriet with crossed arms as if he was searching deep into her soul. The last time Harriet had seen Robert, he was in the forest where Susan attacked him.

While Billy and Mickey pretended to be bears, Harriet's and Robert's eyes locked together. Harriet squirmed uncomfortably. Part of her was relieved to see Robert was okay, but another part resented him for sharing part of her secret.

"What happened out in the forest?" Robert asked.

"Not now, Robert," Auntie Helen said. "Let your cousin rest. The important thing is she's safe."

Harriet's brain raced. Robert was the only person in this room who had seen Susan. He'd seen the wild side of her friend, but he knew she hadn't been with bears. Robert had come looking for her. She wished she knew if he came because he cared or if it was duty. Harriet needed to tell someone about the cabin in the woods. She had to collect evidence for the police. Could she trust Robert? Most of her mind was screaming no, but she wasn't sure who else she could trust. No adult would believe her. Annie was always so busy with her brothers and sisters she may not even come to the hospital. Perhaps Robert was the best ally she had.

"Come now," Auntie Helen said. "That's enough for one day. Harriet, we'll come back tomorrow. Rest and get better. Is there anything you want?"

"My journal and a pen," Harriet said.

"To write your fantastical tale," Robert said.

"Yes," Harriet replied. "The Gazette will pay good money for it."

They stared at each other until the silence became awkward.

"Robert, leave your cousin alone," Auntie Helen said. "Any writing can wait until we visit tomorrow."

She ushered the boys out of the room.

"Robert," Harriet called.

Robert turned to Harriet.

"I have to ask you something."

Robert walked slowly to Harriet's bedside.

"You know I wasn't with bears. The truth is wilder and more fantastical. There are strange things going on here. I think Dr. Smith is working with Herr Schmidt."

Robert rolled his eyes.

"I don't know their plan but, if you help me, I'll move out of your house, so I don't bother you anymore. Come back tonight. There's more going on here than a haunted hospital and being looked after by bears."

Robert looked down at Harriet. Turned on his heels, walked out and closed the door behind him.

Harriet stared up at the ceiling. She was alone. There was no way Robert would come back and help. She knew what she had to do. Now, she had to figure out how she could do it.

# CHAPTER SIXTEEN
## GHOSTS

Every time her hospital door opened, Harriet pretended she was asleep. Orderlies left soup and bread by her bed. She ate to make sure she kept her strength up. Time inched by. Nurses took her pulse and temperature. Harriet guessed they did this every hour. Finally, the intense heat of the day faded. A cool evening breeze drifted through the open window. Someone came in and pulled a blanket over her.

"Let her sleep," the doctor said. "I'll change her dressing in the morning."

Daylight gradually turned to yellow, orange, red, deep indigo and finally turned black.

Harriet's heart pounded. Slowly, she pushed her covers away. The rustle of the crisp linen sheets sounded as loud as an air-raid siren over London. Harriet created a sling by cupping her injured arm at the elbow. Her bare feet touched the polished wooden floor. She reached for her gas mask box, walked the few paces to the door, and pressed her ear against it.

Silence. Harriet moved her hand to the doorknob. Her shoulder ached. Her legs felt weak, but her resolve was strong. She opened the door just enough to peer down the hallway. Empty.

Harriet walked quickly. Her white nightgown fluttered. She cursed her aunt for making this choice in nightwear. Robert's dark flannel pajamas would have given her some camouflage. The hospital hallway seemed to go on and on as Harriet tiptoed to the stairs.

Harriet heard footsteps on the gravel driveway. She pressed her body against the wall and peeked around the window frame. Two orderlies carried a stretcher. Someone lay asleep, covered with a blanket. The doctor opened the back of the waiting ambulance.

If only she had a camera. Harriet needed evidence that the doctor was taking his next victim to the cabin in the forest. No one would believe her without proof.

Harriet watched until the ambulance drove away into the night. At least the doctor wouldn't catch her out of her room. She hurried on, found the stairs and climbed them to her mother's floor.

Every barefoot step sounded like drumbeats in her ears. It felt as if someone was following her. She glanced over her shoulder. All she saw were dark oil portraits staring back at her from their place on the wall. Breathing was difficult. The air was thin. Harriet forced it into her lungs. It was like breathing through a straw. She had to get to her mother. Out of the corner of her eye, she spotted a girl outside the window—her white dress fluttered in the wind. Harriet stifled a scream as she dropped to the floor and curled into a ball.

She shook her head and spoke firmly to herself. "There's no such thing as ghosts."

Slowly, she stood up. A girl's eyes stared straight back at her through the dark window, her own eyes. Harriet felt embarrassed. She'd been scared of her own reflection.

With new resolve, she walked to her mom's room. What she found broke Harriet's heart. While her new friend had saved Harriet, her mother had been lying here.

Harriet came close to her mom's bed. Each wheezing inhalation drew her mother's cheeks over protruding skull bones. This was worse than *White Zombie*, the first horror film Harriet had seen. Harriet bent over her mother's skeletal frame, stroked her face and gently kissed her cheek.

"Harriet?"

"Shh! Don't talk. I've brought you something."

"Harriet, is that really you?"

"It's me, Mummy. Lie still. This will make you feel better."

Harriet opened her gas mask box and took some herbs. She searched her memory and prepared the medicine like the old sasquatch—chewing and rolling them in her own mouth before placing them into the cheek of the patient. Harriet wondered if the herbs would work as well when she prepared them.

"Don't swallow this. Just let it sit in your mouth. It'll make you feel better."

"Lie with me."

Harriet looked over her shoulder. The door remained shut. She put the box on the floor, climbed onto the bed and lay down next to her mother's cold thin body.

"I love you," Harriet's mom whispered.

"I love you too."

Harriet lay there breathing for the two of them, warming her mother's body with her own. When she was sure her mother was asleep, Harriet peeled herself away and prayed the herbs would work. In sleep, her mom's breathing seemed calmer, but there wasn't the dramatic change Harriet had felt in her own body.

"Get better," Harriet whispered as she left her mom's room.

The hallway seemed colder and darker than before. Stars twinkled in the night sky and the moon illuminated the empty gravel driveway. She stared at the moon, wondering if she needed to get Susan to mix the herbs and work sasquatch magic for her mom.

Then, out of the shadows, stood a man in a bowler hat. He

raised a hand to his face. Harriet panicked. She was out of her room, in the middle of the night, in a haunted hospital. She needed time to think. Harriet ran into her mom's room, closed the door and pressed it shut with her good shoulder.

# CHAPTER SEVENTEEN
## THE BOWLER HAT

"Harriet."

A whisper penetrated the door. Every cell in Harriet's body shook. "Harriet, it's me. Open the door."

Harriet took a deep breath. She knew the voice. Her muscles relaxed and allowed her brain to process what was happening. If there really were a ghost in the hallway, a door wouldn't stop it. Slowly, Harriet turned the doorknob, opened the door and peeked through.

There stood Robert, in a man's suit many sizes too big for him, with the sleeves folded back and the waist pulled in with a belt. On his head sat a bowler hat, and under it Harriet could see the smirk on her cousin's face. She pulled him into her mom's room and closed the door behind him.

"Robert Edward Davis, what are you doing?"

"You thought I was an actual ghost. OoooOOOOOooooo!"

"I did not! I just wasn't expecting to see anyone."

Harriet felt relieved the darkness made it impossible for Robert to see her reddening face as embarrassment swept through and heated her body.

"But you told me to come."

"Why the Halloween costume?"

"I'm not meant to be here, so I needed a disguise. And I'd prefer to be in bed so this had better be good."

Harriet's brain was whirring. She didn't trust Robert but here he was, in the middle of the night, asking her to explain what was happening. She opened the box slung over her shoulder and pulled out some herbs.

"You know a bear didn't attack you, don't you?"

Robert nodded his head.

"It was a sasquatch," Harriet continued. "When the doctor shot me, Susan…"

"Susan?"

"That's her name."

"A girl?"

"Stop interrupting and let me tell the story. Susan took me to an ancient sasquatch who healed my shoulder, fever and pain. I'm hoping herbs will heal Mom as well."

He shook his head as if he were trying to rattle his thoughts until they fell into place. "Hang on a second, you'd better tell me just what happened to you out there."

Harriet told Robert about running away, following giant footsteps to the cabin in the forest. How she planned to shelter there until the rain stopped, but the doctor and orderlies arrived with someone on a stretcher. Robert frowned as Harriet told him about the herbs and experiments, the chase through the forest and her overnight stay with Susan Sasquatch.

"The wild animal that attacked me?" Robert asked.

"My friend." Harriet lifted her chin in the air. No one was going to insult Susan.

"The bear."

"You know it wasn't a bear. Call her Bigfoot, Smelly Sasquatch, or whatever you want. And she wasn't attacking you, she was protecting me."

Robert stood and scrutinized Harriet like the young attorney in *On Trial*. He looked for the point in the story where he could cross-examine her and reveal it as bogus. Harriet's skin crawled.

She skipped the section about seeing the other sasquatches and the leader hit Susan. It seemed so unlikely. Even Harriet was unsure whether this part was a dream. Harriet jumped to the cave with the old Sasquatch, the herbs, her conversation with the doctor, and the visit from the German shopkeeper. She told Robert about the herbs she'd given her mother and how she hoped they'd be the miracle cure.

Robert remained silent for a long time.

"You're insane," he finally said. "I have been up all night. And for what! A fairy tale about creatures living in the forest. A mythological beast with more knowledge than a doctor. A doctor, according to you, who's experimenting in a cabin in the forest and conspiring with a German spy. Do you really think I was born yesterday?"

Robert turned to the door. He didn't believe her, which meant he wouldn't help. She didn't know how she would do it all by herself.

"Harriet, Robert, is that you?" Harriet's mom said.

Harriet's heart fell. Her mom's voice was still barely audible through the high-pitched whistle of her wheezing.

"Shhh Mom. You need to rest."

Harriet's mom raised her hand to her mouth, spat out the herbs and held them to the light creeping around the blackout blinds.

Doubt crept into Harriet's mind. The herbs had worked instantaneously for her. Harriet wondered if she'd missed a vital ingredient. She searched her memory and wondered if she'd stolen all the herbs she needed. She crossed her fingers and hoped the mixture would do some good.

"Leave them," Harriet said. "It's a new medicine. You'll be better soon."

Robert shook his head and opened the door. "Are you sure you didn't hit your head in the forest? You're delusional."

Early morning light flooded the room as Harriet watched her cousin walk away. Then, the sound of wheels on gravel filled the silence. Harriet rushed to the hallway window. Against the pink sky and silhouetted trees, she could see the ambulance driving up to the hospital entrance.

"Robert, you don't have to believe me. You can see for yourself."

They stood side by side and watched as three men got out of the vehicle. They lifted someone on a stretcher from the back of the ambulance and walked into the hospital.

"You see! It's the doctor coming back from the forest. There it is. Proof. Now you have to believe me!"

"What I see is a doctor bringing a patient to a hospital. There is nothing unusual about that."

Her stomach knotted up. "But he took the patient out of here last night."

"So you say. Now, I'm going home, and I'll probably arrive just in time for my alarm clock to go off."

She grabbed his arm, desperate to make him listen. "Robert, I know you don't believe me…"

"You don't say!"

"Please come back later. See if the doctor leaves tonight. Follow him on your bike. See for yourself."

Robert walked away without saying another word. Harriet blew her mother a kiss, closed the bedroom door and walked back to her own room. She laid her head on her pillow. She had to think of a way to convince someone, anyone of the truth. Susan attacked Robert. He knew she wasn't with bears, but he didn't believe the incredible events she'd lived through. There was no way to convince this small town about its dark secrets. Not even her cousin believed her. It was a child's story against a doctor and the radio broadcasts about her rescue from the paws of bears. She had to find a way.

# CHAPTER EIGHTEEN
# THE BULLET

In the silence of her hospital room, Harriet's brain buzzed. Until someone believed her, the doctor would continue to take patients to the forest. She had to gather evidence and get it to the police. Her shoulder ached. She placed the hand of her good arm over the gauze covering the bullet wound. She longed for Susan's soothing poultice, the warm comforting pool, the herbs that eased the pain and those that slowed her breathing.

Harriet placed her feet on the floor and walked the few steps to the dresser. She opened the tin box and lifted out her gas mask. The herb mix was dry and stuck to the bottom. She wondered whether the herbs were working for her mom. Harriet thought about the cave and the old sasquatch.

Harriet felt confused. *I must've combined the herbs differently.* The medicine had worked instantaneously for her. She pictured the plants being chewed and rolled. She'd done the same, but her spit wasn't sasquatch spit. That had to be the key—the missing ingredient.

The ancient wisdom amazed her. She never thought that something mixed with saliva would be good for you. Animal mouths were full of germs. Yet, what do cats do when they've been in a fight? They lick their wounds and make them better.

Harriet turned her head, poked out her tongue and tried to reach the covered wound. The clean, dry gauze made the tip of her tongue tingle. Whatever healing powers Susan and her fellow sasquatches understood, humans had long forgotten.

She touched the herbs with the tip of her finger and placed the bitter plant mix in her mouth. The pain in her shoulder eased a little. It was a poor second to the medicine in the forest.

"No more for me," she promised herself. "I have to save this for Mom and mix it with sasquatch spit."

Harriet walked to the window. She could see a young nurse pushing a man in a wheelchair. Nearby, the doctor stood with a soldier in uniform.

Herr Schmidt's truck came up the driveway and paused by the doctor. Harriet watched as the German shopkeeper greeted the man in uniform, then the doctor. They talked for a while then the Herr Schmidt drove around the building to the hospital kitchens. Whatever was going on, Harriet knew they were in this together.

She had to get news to the police and make them believe her. But first, she had to see Susan and get the miracle cure for her mom.

The day passed slowly. Harriet was the model patient. She ate all of her beef broth and bread. Then, when her aunt came in with the doctor, Harriet saw lightness in their faces she'd not seen since they took her mother in the ambulance. Auntie Helen took a pile of nightgowns out of her basket and placed them in the dresser.

"I don't think she'll need all of those," the doctor said. He ran his finger over the indentation on the gas mask tin. "The bullet must've ricocheted off this. Carrying your gas mask saved you, young lady. You had a lucky escape, a flesh wound and no infections."

Harriet's aunt then placed a bottle of milk and a cookie tin on the dresser.

"Harriet can have these, can't she Doctor?" Auntie Helen said.

"Hmm, I'd better check they're fit for human consumption," the doctor said.

Auntie Helen laughed as the doctor took a cookie and bit into it. Harriet's eyes narrowed. Her aunt fell for his charm and wit. Harriet had to expose the doctor's true nature and his experiments in the forest.

"Oh, this is good! And no hidden escape plans."

"The only secret is the recipe, and as town baker, I'm not about to give that up soon," Auntie Helen said.

Harriet did not take her eyes off the doctor.

"How's Mom?" Harriet asked.

"She's a little better today," Auntie Helen said.

"Still weak," the doctor clarified. "But she's taken a step in the right direction."

The doctor smiled at Auntie Helen, and she blushed.

"There must be something in the air," he said. "Both Hall patients are showing signs of improvement. Let's look at this wound of yours."

Harriet felt confused as she pulled her nightgown from her shoulder to reveal the dressing. It was a relief to hear the plant mix was easing her mom's suffering, but Harriet questioned whether the recovery would last. Harriet winced as the doctor peeled the gauze away.

"Slowly does it," the doctor said. "I don't want to open up the wound."

Auntie Helen looked away. As soon as she averted her eyes, the doctor ripped the dressing off. Harriet screamed in pain and watched a small trickle of blood run down her arm. The doctor caught the red liquid in the gauze he held to the wound.

"Well, I'd better be going," Auntie Helen said. "Goodness knows what the house will be like with Robert in charge. I'll drop by tomorrow and bring some currant buns."

Auntie Helen hurried from the room. Harriet and the doctor

sat in silence while the heavy wooden door swung closed behind her. Her heart was beating double time. They were alone. The doctor took a bottle of antiseptic lotion from his bag and poured some onto a piece of clean linen.

"Call out and I'll tell them you're a coward, a little girl not brave enough to have your wound cleaned," the doctor warned.

He took the gauze from her shoulder and pushed the soaking cloth into her open wound.

Harriet wanted to scream against the burning sting. Instead, she clenched her teeth and glared at the doctor.

"Who were you with in the forest?" the doctor asked. "Who treated you? What did they put on it?"

With every question, the doctor applied extra pressure to Harriet's shoulder, and she bit down harder.

"You will tell me. You can do it now or later. But the sooner you talk, the better for everyone."

Harriet's eyes stung, and pain shot all the way down her arm to her fingers. She refused to talk. She repeated the war slogan in her mind. *Careless talk cost lives. Careless talk costs lives.* She'd seen the doctor talking with the shopkeeper with her own eyes. The doctor would share any information with Herr Schmidt, then Adolf Hitler. He was German after all was said and done. It was her duty to stay silent.

"Stubbornness is not an attractive quality in one so young," the doctor said. "Do you know how many lives I could save? Soldiers get shot all the time. The lucky ones die quickly. They maim others for life—infections set in, limbs get amputated, they leave men blind. But here you are, bright and breezy, refusing to help the war effort. Who are you trying to protect? The animal that attacked your cousin, your kin, your own flesh and blood? Your loyalties are all wrong."

Harriet thought about her secret getting to the Germans. She had to keep quiet. She would not tell the doctor about Susan or the old medicine creature in the mountains. Pain forced blood to her head. Harriet wanted to call out, open her mouth and release any sound that would stop the torture.

Just as Harriet could bear the pain no longer, the bedroom door swung open. Harriet and the doctor spun their heads to see Auntie Helen, breathless and flushed, standing at the door. The doctor instantly stopped pressing so hard on her shoulder and Harriet felt like she could just hug her aunt.

"I almost forgot," Auntie Helen said. "Robert asked me to give you this."

Auntie Helen took an empty bullet shell from her basket and handed it to Harriet.

"'Exhibit A' he called it. Boys! I don't know why he thinks you'd want a spent rifle shell," Auntie Helen said. "Now listen to the doctor, be brave and you'll be home before we know it."

Auntie Helen kissed Harriet's forehead and hurried out of the room. The brass shell felt smooth and cold in Harriet's fingers. She brought it to her nose. There was a faint smell of gunpowder mixed with earth. A smile bubbled to the surface from deep within Harriet's body. Robert had been to the place where Susan attacked him and she'd been shot. He'd searched for the shell, evidence. This was Robert's way of admitting the truth about the attack. She closed her fist around the bullet and remained silent.

The doctor dressed Harriet's wound without another word. Then, before he left, he turned to her.

"Just imagine if your father arrived in this hospital, injured from the war," he said. "You'd do everything in your power to heal him. Think about it. Your father and tens of thousands of other fathers, brothers, uncles and cousins are dying, and why? So, you can protect Big Foot. The brute who'd have killed your cousin if it weren't for me. Human beings or a wild animal? That's your choice. I can save lives, if you'll show me what the beast showed you. Just think about that."

# CHAPTER NINETEEN
## CAUGHT

The hours until nightfall felt like an eternity of math lessons. Finally, the sky turned pink and purple, and then red. Harriet's door opened, and a nurse bustled about, taking Harriet's pulse and temperature. She tucked Harriet into bed and closed the blackout blinds.

Harriet waited and listened. All was quiet. She pulled the sheet off her body, peeked out between the blind and window, and watched until the sky blackened. She knew it wasn't safe to venture out until the doctor left for the cabin. Minutes crept by. Harriet felt her way to the dresser and took out the last cookie. She nibbled the edges and waited. Into the silence cut the noise of wheels on gravel. Harriet raced back to her lookout post. The ambulance pulled up in front of the hospital. She watched as the orderlies got out and walked into the building. A few minutes later, Harriet squinted through the darkness as they loaded a stretcher into the back of the ambulance and three men climbed into the cab. The coast was clear. The doctor had left for the night.

Harriet put her cookie on the dresser, collected the cake tin and a soupspoon, and hurried out of the room. Each bare footstep seemed to echo throughout the building. Each stair that squeaked made her cringe. She tried the front door. Locked. She thought of Robert's route through the kitchen. In the darkness, she found the dining room then tiptoed past the giant cooker, not daring to breathe. Finally, she felt the back door, pushed against it and found herself in the cool, night air.

Garbage cans, boxes, and the doctor's old Ford Angler sat in the courtyard. Harriet ran past them and onto the soft, dewy grass in front of the hospital. She looked down at her white nightgown in the light. If anyone saw her, she'd look like the child ghost from the nurses' logbook. She glanced back to the hospital. The blackout blinds were all drawn. The building and its inhabitants slept.

She raced to the road by the lake and turned onto a small path that led to the forest. Harriet's eyes adjusted to the dim moonlight shining through the trees. Finally, in the mouth of a cave, Harriet spotted a clump of the magic herb. She pinched the leaf and placed it on her tongue. The fine hairs tickled her tongue, and the spicy flavour sent a welcome, soothing sensation down her throat. *This is it.* The plant on its own was better than nothing. With some luck, she'd see Susan and get her to chew it into medicine. Harriet took her soupspoon from the cake tin and dug in the moist soil. Long tuber-like roots came up in her hands. She looked around for a pool of water to wash off the dirt. Nothing looked clean. Mud oozed through her toes as she walked. She had dirt on her nightgown. She tried to lift the gown with her good hand but only got more dirt on the material. The hairs on her skin bristled. Her body shivered despite the warm air on her skin. Someone was bound to find her out of her hospital room in the middle of the night. She heard an owl hoot and coyotes howled in the distance. Harriet turned back to the lake. She needed to wash the herbs before mashing them to a pulp.

As Harriet approached the lake, she saw a flashing light. She hid behind a tree and wished her nightclothes were black. The flashing stopped. Harriet peeped around the tree. Flash, flash,

flash, flash. Sometimes long, others quick—Morse code? Harriet watched. Her heart raced. Someone was sending a signal. Or maybe the message wasn't for her. Herr Schmidt's spy network could be out here and active. Harriet wondered who else was involved. The doctor had already left for the cabin. There must other spies. Harriet knew her duty was to report them, but she had to get medicine to her mother. The problem now was her white nightie. It would give her away.

There was a pause. Then the flashlight started up again. This time the signal was closer to her. The light seemed to shine directly at her. Harriet searched her memory of the code in Robert's scout book. Quick and slow bursts of light shone directly at the tree where she hid. Dot, dash, dot—R—dash, dash, dash, dash, dash—O—dash, dot, dot, dot—B.

"Robert?" Harriet whispered.

Robert climbed out from under a dinghy lying upside down on the sand and ran across the beach.

"You scared me half to death," Harriet said.

"What are you doing?" Robert asked. "I was coming to the hospital." Robert took his backpack from his shoulders and opened it on the wet sand. "If you're right about the doctor, we have to get evidence."

Robert pulled out his Box Brownie and showed it to Harriet. Then he took out a map showing the lake, town, logging roads and buildings in the forest.

"Where did you get that?"

"I 'borrowed' it from the library. Now where's this cabin?"

"I don't know. If you remember, it was raining, and I was mad at you when I stumbled on it."

Harriet wanted to say she'd been following Susan's footprints but stopped herself. Robert's meeting with the sasquatch hadn't gone well. She didn't want him to give up because Susan terrified him.

"Think. Anything. Talk me through everything you remember," Robert said.

"I left the house and took the path to the lake," Harriet said.

Robert held the flashlight and placed a finger on the map.

"Then I came to a junction and took the smaller path. I crossed a small stream and continued up a steep trail," Harriet continued.

"You must have come along here," Robert said.

Robert laughed.

"What's funny?"

"I asked the search party if we should look for you up here and someone said, 'No, it's too steep for a girl.'"

"Who? Was it the doctor?"

"I don't think so. It was all frantic. Maybe the new police chief."

"Or Herr Schmidt?"

"He was definitely looking for you. Oh, golden girl who gets Stollen brought to her bedside."

Frustration rose in Harriet's chest. This sounded like the Robert of old—superior and sarcastic—not the boy sitting on the beach in the middle of the night holding a flashlight and map.

"Robert, can't you see? The doctor and Herr Schmidt are working together. They'll get the medicine to the enemy." Harriet opened the cake tin. With these, German troops could fight on and on. This war will never end."

"If what you're saying is true, we have to stop them." Robert leaned over the map and put his serious face on. "What happened next?"

"It was raining, and I saw a cabin. I thought I'd shelter there until the rain stopped."

"And make us all come looking for you. Didn't it cross your mind just to come home?"

Harriet ignored her cousin's comment. "Then the ambulance came up the logging road."

"You must have been here." He pointed to a spot. Robert stood up and folded the map.

"What are you going to do?" Harriet asked.

"I'm going to collect evidence. If you're right, the police need to know about this."

"I'll come," Harriet said.

Robert looked at Harriet's bare feet and the way she cradled her aching shoulder.

"You're a liability," Robert said. "Get yourself strong. I'm going to get some photos and take them to the police station. I'm sure they'll want to talk with you tomorrow."

Harriet watched Robert cross the sand, jump on his bike and pedal away. She wanted to go with him, but knew it made sense for her to stay behind. She turned back to the lake, smiled at the moonlight sparkling on the surface, washed the herbs and placed most of them back in the tin to take to her mom. On the beach, she found two smooth rocks. Placed a plant between them, ground them, then put them into her mouth to chew. Once they were a fine pulp, Harriet peeled the dressing from her shoulder, removed the mush from her mouth, placed it on the wound and replaced the dressing. A cool tingling eased some pain in her shoulder. The effect wasn't as dramatic as the time Susan had applied the herbs—confirmation of the miracle that lay in a sasquatch's mouth.

The smell of wet dog crept into her nostrils. Harriet turned and stared into the forest.

"Hello?" Harriet whispered.

Long hair-covered fingers appeared from behind a tree, closely followed by Susan's familiar smile. Harriet dropped her tin, spoon and herbs and threw herself into the sasquatch's arms.

"You're still here," Harriet said.

Susan placed her skin-covered palm on Harriet's shoulder and sniffed at the dressing. She peeled away the tape and gently lifted the herbs. Her long black tongue licked the red disinfectant and spat it on the ground. Susan took the herbs from Harriet's shoulder, chewed them, and put them back on the wound.

Harriet opened her box and held out a clump of herbs. She

looked into Susan's enormous eyes with the pleading look of a starving beggar. Susan took the plants, chewed them and spat them out into Harriet's outstretched hand.

"Susan, I can't stay. I have to get these to my mother. Thank you," Harriet said. She was so grateful this creature was helping her and wondered how she could ever repay this kind of friendship.

She kissed Susan on the soft fur above her protruding eye sockets and got up to leave. Susan tilted her head to one side. They stared at each other. Susan was the first to break the stalemate. She got up, walked back to the forest and sat alone on a rock. Harriet felt torn in two. She needed to get the medicine to her mother and wished Susan had a family to go back to. She hoped it wasn't her fault that Susan was alone. The memory of the sasquatch hitting Susan felt like a recurring nightmare. Harriet didn't even know if the old sasquatch had taken pity on her or Susan.

Harriet wanted to take Susan home, to look after her like she used to do with stray cats, but something told her the sasquatch belonged in the forest. Their friendship only existed in the space between their worlds. She wished this gap would lessen but something inside Harriet told her she had to accept the friendship as it was, with all its limitations.

"I'll come back," Harriet said. "Promise."

Harriet turned and walked back to the hospital.

No one stopped her as she crept back through the kitchen, up to the second floor, and opened the door to her mother's room. Harriet kissed her mother.

"Harriet? Is that you?"

"Yes, but don't talk."

"Did I dream it or did you give me alternative medicine?"

"It was me, but hush, rest. I have more for you. This will work wonders."

Harriet picked up an herb ball.

"Put this in your mouth and keep it there for as long as you can. There's another one here. Go back to sleep and I'll come back to visit you soon."

Harriet leaned over and kissed her mother's brow.

"Harriet, I will get better. You know that, don't you?"

She felt her throat grow tight. "Yes, I do." And she was believing it for real.

Harriet tiptoed into the hall and closed the door silently. A smile crept across her face. The medicine was complete. It'd work, she'd seen Susan, and Robert was collecting evidence to take to the police. Everything was falling into place.

Then, from out of the darkness, she felt a hand cover her mouth and another press down on her shoulder.

"Touching, very touching," the doctor said. "Now, you're going to tell me all about your jaunt into the forest and exactly what you've given your mother."

Pain shot down Harriet's arm and her legs buckled as the doctor dug his fingers into her wound. He forced her along the hallway, down the stairs and back to her room.

"Call out and I'll sedate you."

He flung Harriet onto her bed.

"When I get back, you'd better be ready to talk."

He left the room and locked the door behind him. Harriet raced to the window and saw the ambulance drive from the direction of the delivery dock to the front of the hospital. It confused Harriet. She'd seen it drive away and not return. She wondered what Robert would find when he got to the cabin. The doctor had either gone to the cabin and returned or had never left. But Harriet saw three men leave the hospital—the two orderlies and the doctor, or at least someone who looked like the doctor. She had to get to the police.

Harriet pulled back the blackout blinds and opened her window. She was about to climb out when she heard voices. She flattened her body against the wall and peeked around. There in the darkness was someone on the stretcher. Harriet willed her eyes to adjust to the darkness. In the moonlight, Harriet recognized the shape of the patient. It was her mother!

The men loaded up the stretcher into the ambulance and walked back into the hospital. The coast was clear. Slowly and painfully, Harriet climbed out the window. A key turned in the lock and before her entire body was outside, the doctor grabbed her by both arms and yanked her back into the room. The force tore the scab off Harriet's wound. Blood seeped through the dressing and onto Harriet's white nightgown.

"You'll never get away with this," Harriet said.

"Get away with what?" the doctor asked.

"Experimenting on patients in the forest."

"Is that what I'm doing? I was thinking I was doing my job, making medicine and healing people."

At that moment, the two orderlies filled the doorframe. Fear seized Harriet's mind and body. These were the men who had loaded her mother into the ambulance.

"Gentlemen," the doctor said. "This young lady thinks I'm a mad scientist, performing dark and dangerous experiments on people in the forest."

The orderlies looked from the doctor to Harriet.

"Don't just stand there. Gag her. Shut her up. She's delusional," the doctor said. "Hold her down. She needs to sleep."

The men grabbed Harriet and carried her to her bed. They pinned down her arms and legs. The doctor took a large needle from his bag and stabbed it into Harriet's arm.

"I'll just borrow this tin until morning," the doctor said.

Harriet's limbs went limp, her eyelids heavy, and although she tried to scream, no voice came out. She lay, unable to rescue her mother, as darkness engulfed her body.

## CHAPTER TWENTY
## GOING HOME

"Good morning, sleepyhead," Auntie Helen said.

Harriet forced her eyes open. The room spun, and she felt her body was full of thick London smog. She closed her eyes again and willed them to work.

"Come on now. You can't sleep all day."

Harriet recognized the fake chirpiness in the doctor's voice. "This young lady has made a remarkable recovery. You can take her home as soon as you can get her up and dressed."

Harriet sat up and stared at him. She was about to say something when Billy and Mickey jumped on the bed to hug their cousin.

"Gently boys, gently," Auntie Helen said. "Remember, Harriet was hurt just two days ago."

"Robert said he found the bullet and gave it to you," Billy said.

"Can we see it?" Mickey asked.

Harriet reached out her good arm to the dresser and noticed her cake tin back in its place. She picked up the bullet and held it up towards the doctor's face.

"Wow!" Billy said.

Mickey grabbed the bullet and accidentally pulled the sheet from Harriet's shoulder.

"Is that blood?" Auntie Helen asked.

"The wound opened a little last night when our patient tried to do too much too soon," the doctor replied. "You'll have to make sure this little monkey gets plenty of rest."

Harriet opened the tin, found a cinnamon bun, but no herbs. She handed the treat to Billy who divided it in two, kept the bigger section and handed the smaller bit to Mickey.

"Boys, wait outside the room while Harriet gets changed," Auntie Helen said. "I've brought some clean clothes for you. I'll have to add getting this blood out of your nightie my list of things to do."

"Doctor," Harriet said. "Can I see my mom before we go?"

"Of course. She was resting when I saw her this morning. Come on up when you're ready. I'm heading there now to see if she's awake."

Harriet watched as the doctor left the room.

"Auntie Helen," Harriet said. "I think the doctor is taking his patients into the forest at night."

She drew back, shocked. "Harriet! What a thing to say! Why would he do that?"

Harriet grabbed her arm. "He's testing medicine on them. He sedates them and takes them to a cabin."

"Harriet Hall, stop these stories right now!"

"They're not stories. Believe me. Dr. Smith shot me, then sasquatches gave me medicine. That's why I got better so quickly. Now the doctor wants to know the secrets of the forest." Harriet's insides churned. She had to make Auntie Helen believe her.

"And where is this medicine now?"

"He found me giving some to Mom, forced me back into my room, stole the herbs I had and took Mom away in an ambulance to do his experiments."

Auntie Helen shook her head. "My, my, you are excitable.

And you're under doctor's orders to rest. Perhaps you should write all these stories down. Stories of espionage and horror sell well in times of war. But Harriet, you can't spoil a good man's name. Dr. Smith helps our town. He rescued you from a bear, healed your wound, and is making your mom better. No more of your stories. Let's get you changed and go to see your mother."

Harriet pulled on her skirt, socks and blouse. Auntie Helen gathered up the spare nightgowns, helped Harriet put on her shoes and went to find Billy and Mickey. Together, they climbed the stairs to the second floor.

"Is this where you'll see the ghosts?" Billy asked.

"Billy Davis, there are no such thing as ghosts," Auntie Helen said.

"But Harriet said ghosts haunt the hospital," Mickey said.

"She did, did she? Perhaps it's time to learn you can't trust everything you're told by your cousin."

Auntie Helen gave Harriet a look as they reached her mother's bedroom door. For adults to believe her, she was going to have to collect a lot of evidence. She hoped Robert had captured the doctor on film and taken the photos to the police.

Inside the room, Harriet's mother was propped up on pillows. She took a dark ball from her cheek. Harriet ran to her mother and hugged her. The herbs alone had helped, but mixed in Susan's mouth the effect was sensational.

"Careful," the doctor said. "Don't drop the medicine. It's working miraculously."

Harriet met the doctor's eyes. Her mother's wheezing was quieter, and her eyes could focus. Harriet felt waves of relief and anger wash over her. Her mother was getting better, even if the doctor was taking the credit for it. She had to get adults to take her seriously. No one believed her about the doctor experimenting in the forest at night or that the medicine came right from the forest's fauna and flora.

"You're looking better," Auntie Helen said.

"A bit better today than yesterday," Harriet's mom said. "I think I'll try some broth today. Build up my strength."

"That's the spirit," the doctor said. "We'll have you home in no time. Now, I have two young ladies who need to rest. Mrs. Davis, time to take Harriet home. We'll take good care of Mrs. Hall, and maybe you could bring one of your bread rolls for her when you visit tomorrow. And a cinnamon bun for me."

With that Auntie Helen gave her sister-in-law a kiss on the cheek, gathered her things and walked to the door. Harriet looked at the doctor, hugged her mother and followed her aunt and cousins out of the room. She had to know what evidence Robert had found.

# CHAPTER TWENTY-ONE
## THE PLAN

"Harriet," Annie called from the back gate. "I heard you were home. Thank goodness you're okay."

Harriet smiled. She had been home less than fifteen minutes. News traveled fast in this town. Annie gave Harriet a careful hug and sat beside her under the Douglas fir. Harriet put down her notebook and pencil next to Robert's scout book, that lay on the grass, open to a page about forest plants.

"Where's your sister and all your brothers?" Harriet asked.

"Home with mom. She said I could come and see how you are. What are you doing?"

Harriet picked up the scout book and showed Annie the illustrations. She pointed to one labelled 'plantain.'

"These are the roots that healed my shoulder so quickly," Harriet said. "The doctor kept taking them off and putting disinfectant on instead. I need to get to the forest and find some more. This plant doesn't sting, and even the doctor commented on how quickly I got better."

Harriet thought about telling Annie about Susan's healing spit, but decided it was too complicated. She put the scout book back on the grass.

"Do you know where Robert is?" Harriet asked.

"He told me he was taking 'incriminating evidence' to Brennan Police Station," Annie said. "What's going on? One minute you were lost in the forest, then there was talk of you being shot, and a crazy story on the news about you being looked after by bears. Did you see yourself in the paper? Now, you're talking about medicine from the forest and Robert is playing detective."

Annie handed Harriet a copy of *The Three Mills Gazette*. The headline announced: "Doctor Rescues Kids from Bear Attack." It was time to set the record straight. Harriet filled Annie in on everything that had happened since she ran away. It felt good to tell the whole story to someone who didn't interrupt. Annie sat in dismay as Harriet listed the doctor, Herr Schmidt and the orderlies as enemy agents. She told her friend the part they each played in the plan to get secret medical treatments to Germany.

"So," Harriet concluded. "We have to expose them, before they kill someone, or worse, get miracle cures to the Third Reich."

At that moment, the back gate swung open and Robert came in, pushing the baker's bike. His shirt was stained with sweat. He dropped the bike onto the grass.

"Say hello to Sherlock Holmes," Robert said, striking a pose. "Ace detective and exposer of the truth."

Harriet's neck hair bristled. Robert's confidence wound her up.

"Did you take the photos to the police?"

"Ah, dear Watson, there is nothing more stimulating than a case where everything goes against you."

"What happened?"

"The photos won't be ready until tomorrow."

"But you got photos of the ambulance and the doctor taking Mom to the cabin."

"No, the cabin was empty," Robert replied.

Harriet felt her shoulders slump. "I told you to hide and wait."

"I have to get up at six o'clock! You can wait in the forest, at night, alone. I got some sleep."

"What evidence did you get?" Annie asked.

"The cabin was full of herb jars, notebooks, mortar and pestle, and a Bunsen burner. It looked like Dr. Frankenstein's laboratory. I took long exposures of everything."

"That may be enough," Annie said.

"No, it won't," Harriet said, frustrated. "I've already tried to tell the truth. No one will believe kids' words against a grown-up, a doctor and pillar of the community."

"Then what do you suggest, smarty pants," Robert said.

"We have to catch them in the act," Harriet said. "They'll be back there tonight."

"But the doctor, Herr Schmidt, and two orderlies are involved," Annie said. "How can three kids beat four adults?"

"I have a plan," Harriet said. "Annie, you're going to delay the doctor."

"How?" Robert and Annie asked together.

"Make your mother call the doctor to your house so Robert and I can reach the cabin before him."

Annie's face scrunched up. "But I'm not sick."

"Fake it."

"How?"

Harriet ticked off the points on her fingers. "The trick is to start early, go home saying you're tired and have a sore throat. You'll be given hot lemon and cod liver oil. Later, play with your food at the dinner table and ask to go to bed early. Then, when you hear the radio playing the eight o'clock news, do as many push-ups as possible until you're burning up and breathless, jump back into bed, call your mother, shiver and say you're cold. She'll feel your forehead and call for the doctor.

"That'll give Robert and me time to get to the cabin before the doctor," Harriet said.

"Harriet, I'm not sure about this," Annie said. "What if Mom doesn't believe me?"

"You need to make her believe you. Just think of what will happen if they can heal all the Germans around the world from their gunshot wounds. Someone, who the doctor can send back into battle, could kill your dad."

"Okay, I'll do it," Annie said, standing up straighter.

"And what are you planning for us?" Robert asked.

"I'm going to catch the doctor red-handed and you'll get everything on film."

Harriet looked at the astonished faces in front of her. "First, we'll lure the doctor into a trap. He'll come for me because he knows that I have the missing ingredient. Once we have caught the doctor, Robert, you'll take photos. Evidence of Dr. Smith getting seized will be enough to bring the police. You can come back with an officer to rescue me. That's when we can reveal the full extent of the crimes going on right under everyone's noses. Now, do we all know what to do?"

There was a moment of silence while Annie and Robert took in the crazy scheme.

"I've run out of film," Robert said.

"And I have to go home," Annie added. "Mom said I wasn't to tire you out. Don't you think we should wait a couple of days?"

Harriet clenched her teeth. If she was going to save the world, she needed help. "No way. The doctor already knows too much, we don't know how long he'll hang around. We have to do this tonight. Annie, let's see your pretend illness."

Annie coughed and rubbed her throat. Harriet showed her how to droop her eyelids and hang her head to one side. Then she detailed the rest of the plan. When she got to the end, Harriet turned to Annie.

"Okay, let's catch these German spies. Auntie Helen usually goes to bed at nine o'clock, sometimes earlier. We can sneak out of the house after that. Keep the doctor at your house as long as possible."

Robert and Harriet watched Annie leave. She got to the gate, waved her hand, then dropped it to her side and slumped home. The first part of the plan was in place.

"Can I say again, I have no more film?"

"Don't worry, we'll put it on your mom's account at the general store and pay for it when I'm paid by The Gazette for my exclusive story. Let's ask if we can get ice cream to celebrate my release from hospital."

Harriet enjoyed being in charge and ordering Robert around. She started writing and rewriting her article in her head. "Harriet Hall, evacuee from London, uncovers secret military experiments." "Harriet Hall, heroine of the Allied forces exposes doctor as German double agent." "Harriet Hall finds the enemy within and saves the lives of our brothers, fathers, uncles and cousins."

A few minutes later, Harriet, Robert, Billy and Mickey walked past Annie's house.

"Want to come for ice cream?" Harriet asked.

"No thank you," Annie replied.

"What's wrong with you?" Mrs. McLoughlin asked.

"I don't know, just not feeling great," Annie replied and then did the eye droop she'd practiced with Harriet.

"You'd better go on without her," Mrs. McLoughlin said. "And Harriet, good to see you up and about. You gave us all quite a scare."

"Sorry, Mrs. McLoughlin. Didn't mean to worry so many people. Get better soon, Annie."

Harriet walked with her cousins to Herr Schmidt's general store feeling confident her plan was working. They pushed open the fly screen and allowed their eyes to adjust to the dim light inside the cluttered store. Billy and Mickey ran to the ice cream display while Harriet piled her things onto the counter—rope, Box Brownie film and flash bulbs.

"That's quite a collection. What's the plan for all this?" Herr Schmidt asked.

Harriet's mind went blank.

"We're building a tree house," Robert said.

"With film and flash bulbs?"

Herr Schmidt asked too many questions.

"I'm going to take photos and send them to my dad," Robert said. "I've heard soldiers like to know what we're doing back home."

"This war is hard on everyone," Herr Schmidt said with a nod. "Let's pray there's a miracle and the right side wins soon. Now, who is paying for this?"

"Mom said you could take it out of the money you owe us for bread this week. She'll settle any difference when we close shop on Saturday."

Harriet was busy stuffing the loot into her satchel.

"You should let your cousin do that. No heavy lifting for you, young lady."

Robert picked up the bag and moved to the door.

"What about my ice cream?" Billy asked.

"Sure," Robert said. "Four vanilla cones."

Herr Schmidt scooped extra helpings for each of them, then added, "Make sure you build that tree house in your yard. We've all had enough of your forest adventures for one summer."

Harriet and Robert looked at each other. It was time to get out of the shop. Anyone who'd read Agatha Christie knows the bad guys always warn the detective to stay away.

Harriet and Robert grabbed the two small boys' hands and led them quickly out of the shop. As they left, Billy tripped, and his ice cream fell onto the dusty step.

"I want another," he cried.

"Here, have mine," Robert said.

"Did you hear what he said to us?" Harriet hissed.

"Shh! Don't talk about it here," Robert said.

"Are we really building a tree house?" Mickey asked.

"Sure," Robert said.

Harriet turned her head and stared at Robert. She couldn't

believe her cousin would waste time building a tree house when there were matters of national security at stake.

"Our plan goes into action tonight. If it's going to work, we need to figure out how to build a trap," Robert said.

"Exactly, there's no time for building a tree house."

"It'll keep Billy and Mickey busy. We'll practice making the trap and use it to launch planks into the tree. That way, the boys will think the tree house is being made and won't tell my mom about our plan," Robert explained.

Harriet hated Robert taking charge, but had to admit her cousin had some good ideas. She'd lassoed statues. She wasn't helpless with ropes, but she'd never set out to capture a gang of criminals. The idea sent a tingle through her body, a combination of excitement and terror.

All afternoon, Harriet read aloud from Robert's scout guide while he worked on various knots and loops. By dinner, they could both build a tree spring noose trap. Billy and Mickey lost interest, went to dig in the dirt until Robert was ready to launch planks into the tree. Once he'd climbed the Douglas fir, Billy and Mickey would come back, eager to see a plank placed on the end of the trigger stick. That would set the trap in motion, grab the plank and send it flying into the air.

Just as Auntie Helen called them in for dinner, Robert caught a plank.

"Perfect," he said, climbing down from the tree and rolling the rope. "Now all we need to do is wait for the adults to go to bed."

# CHAPTER TWENTY-TWO
## TRAPPED

Harriet lay in bed. Her younger cousins breathed softly in their sleep. Radio sounds floated down the hallway. The clipped tone of the newsreader spoke of London being bombed, the brave Canadians training in Halifax and the need for war bonds to pay for the defeat of tyranny. Auntie Helen's knitting needles clicked together to accompany the grim announcements. Tonight, Harriet would finally get her wish. She would be part of the war, and not just collecting tin foil from chocolate wrappers. She would expose the doctor, his experiments, and his accomplice Herr Schmidt. Her article would prove the German wanted to get secret medical knowledge to the Fuhrer. Her name would be in the papers: "Harriet Hall reveals evil plot."

Robert leaned out of his bunk, picked up his alarm clock, lifted the blackout blind and looked at the time. In the dim evening sunlight, Harriet could see her cousin hold up both hands. Ten minutes to go. Auntie Helen would soon lay down her knitting, turn off the radio and head to bed. Harriet rubbed her sore shoulder. Her heart thumped in her chest. She wondered if Robert could hear it. Her mind drifted randomly to her home in London and horseback riding lessons. Her father used to say she had to let the animals know who's boss. Horses can smell fear. Harriet wondered if the same was true for humans. Robert had a way of spotting weakness. The memory of the raccoon poop made her shudder. She wondered if Robert would keep up his end of the bargain. She hoped she could trust him. With any luck, Annie's mom was about to call the doctor. There were so many unknown factors and all she could do was wait.

Finally, the signature tune played at the end of *The News*, and Auntie Helen's familiar bedtime routine got underway. Squeak. She got up from her armchair. Click. The radio dial was switched off. Her footsteps echoed down the hallway, and Harriet heard her aunt clean her teeth. Next, she walked into the children's bedroom. She pulled covers over Billy, Mickey, Robert and Harriet one at a time, and gave each a kiss on the cheek. Harriet kept her eyes closed until she heard the bedsprings on her aunt's bed.

"One Mississippi, two Mississippi, three Mississippi," Harriet counted in her head. Sixty seconds in one minute. Six hundred in ten. That was the time they'd decided it took Auntie Helen to go to sleep. She was always tired—running the bakery and a house with four children meant she often fell asleep in the sitting room. At least tonight she'd heard the end of the news and then turned in.

Harriet had only reached four hundred and fifty-four when she heard Robert climb down from his bunk. It was too soon.

"Stay there," Robert said. "I'm going to see if Mom's asleep."

There was no way Harriet would let Robert take the lead. This was her plan. She moved to the edge of her bed and winced as she lowered her foot to Billy's bed.

"What are you doing?" Billy asked.

"Just going to the washroom," Harriet said. "Go back to sleep."

Billy turned over, pulled his sheet to his chin and went back to sleep. Harriet didn't dare breathe as she pulled on her skirt and shirt. When Robert came back, he was dressed in the same clothes he'd had on earlier. He must have dug them out of the laundry basket.

"Come on," he whispered. "Coast is clear."

They tiptoed down the hallway to the kitchen. Robert took the door handle in his hand and turned it slowly. Harriet grabbed the cake tin out of the larder and left the house. They collected their bag with the rope from behind the Douglas fir. Robert stuffed in his Box Brownie, film and flash, and Harriet held out the tin.

"What do we need that for?" Robert asked.

"Just in case we need protection."

"Will it work?"

"Trust me."

The cousins looked at each other. Harriet knew she couldn't do this by herself. If only Bee was here. She used to do everything Harriet told her to do. Everything was different in Loughlin Mills. Annie and Robert were the best hope she had in this tiny town.

"Come on," Harriet said. "Let's catch the enemy before it's too late."

They left the yard and raced past Annie's house. The doctor's car was already in the driveway. Harriet smiled. Her fake illness trick worked every time.

"There's no time to lose," Harriet said.

They broke into a run just as they felt the first drops of rain on their faces.

"Rain! We don't need rain," Robert said.

"Come on, we have to do this tonight," Harriet said.

"But the camera won't work if it gets wet."

"Wrap it in this," Harriet said.

Harriet pulled her raincoat from the bag. She wouldn't get caught out again.

Robert covered the camera and shoved it back into the bag.

Once they reached the bakery, Robert stuffed the bag into the breadbasket, Harriet climbed onto the back and Robert pedaled out of town. The rain fell heavier and heavier as tarmac turned to loose gravel. The logging track soon resembled a river. Harriet gritted her teeth as they bounced over the rocks. The pain brought tears to her eyes, but the thought of her mother being brought to the cabin kept Harriet from saying anything. They had to reach the cabin and set the trap before the doctor arrived.

"Pedal harder," Harriet said.

"I would if you weren't on the back."

"Let me go ahead. I'll set the trap. You keep the camera safe."

Robert climbed off the bike, took the camera from the bag, put it under his clothes and started running. Harriet held the handlebar with the hand of her good arm and cycled as hard as she could into the night.

Once she reached the cabin, Harriet hid the bike amongst the trees and set to work. There was a sapling close to an enormous fir tree. She used all her weight to bend the young tree and mark where it reached when bowed. Next, she scavenged for the sticks she could use as the trigger, anchor and hook. She hammered them into the ground with a heavy stone. Her shoulder and arm resonated with pain each time she struck a stick. Memories of the doctor, clamping his hand over her wound, swum through her mind. She had to find the strength to do this. She had to stop the doctor.

With the anchor in place, she pulled the rope from the bag. Rain had soaked her to the skin and made her body shake uncontrollably. The rope felt heavy in her hands. With only one good arm, she had to throw it over the branch. She pictured lassoing Nelson, counted to three, and let go.

The rope uncoiled, flew through the air and landed with a wet thud on the ground. Harriet growled with frustration. She could do this. She held the end of the rope in her outstretched hand and coiled the rest around her hand. Rain trickled down her nose. The rope had to go over the branch. Harriet remembered how much easier it was to throw a rope with a heavy knot at the end. She placed the rope on the ground, stood on one end and tied a lasso knot on the other end. The loop circled Harriet's head and gained momentum. Then she took a deep breath, closed her eyes and released the rope.

This time the rope sailed above the branch and came to rest with a long length hanging from either side of the branch. Harriet quickly tied slipknots on either end of the rope. Secured one end to the sapling, pulled it down to the ground, tying the other end to the trigger and covering the loop with leaves. The trap was set. Harriet busied herself with the search for herbs. Despite the lack of moonlight, Harriet could find the plants quickly and easily. It amazed her to think she knew nothing of these medicines until a few days ago. Now, she knew what to look for and what to do once she'd found them. The roots were easy to lift from the sodden ground and she returned to the trap to find Robert huffing up the hill.

"Hide in the trees and set up the camera," Harriet said. "I'm almost ready."

Harriet watched her cousin find a place in the forest, hidden among the thick undergrowth. He unwrapped the camera, placed Harriet's bottle green raincoat over his head and rested his arms on a low branch.

Harriet took up her place by the hidden trap and pounded plantain roots. She added her spittle, knowing it was a poor second to her sasquatch friend's saliva. At least, the medicine would look like the herb ball the doctor had found in her mom's mouth. Harriet's body shook with cold as she stared out into the darkness. The silence was unnerving. She rehearsed the speech she'd prepared: "Hello Dr. Smith, I have something for you. It can be yours, but first, you have something of mine that I want back."

Harriet wondered if anyone would come out on a night like this—a tree could fall, a bomb could explode, and no one would know. She second-guessed what might happen. Perhaps they should have left a note or sent her suspicions to Mr. Gunner at the newspaper. Harriet brought her attention back to the plan. She took the mashed herbs, rolled them into a ball, and waited. Her stomach growled in nervous conversation with her anxious mind. She walked through the steps—Annie had delayed the doctor, Robert was in place with the camera, and she had the herbs that would lure the doctor to the trap. There was no reason for her ideas not to work. Everything was ready. Harriet opened the cake tin to place the medicine inside and protect it from the rain. There, in front of her, sat a cinnamon bun. No one would miss one bite, and it might calm her mind and stomach. She sat on a rock, sunk her teeth into the treat and waited for the ambulance to arrive.

Raindrops pounded on Harriet's body—an external beat echoed by her heart as it tried to leap out of her chest. Then the earthy smell of fresh rain mixed with that of wet dog and skunk cabbage. Harriet froze. It was too soon for Susan to appear. Her part in the plan didn't come until later. Harriet only meant the sasquatch to protect her, to scare away the orderlies if they threatened to hurt her. Now, Susan was here and there was no sign of the doctor or orderlies. Harriet cursed herself for taking out a bun.

"Susan, stay where you are. Stay out of sight. I don't need you," Harriet said. Panic rose in Harriet's chest. Susan's presence changed everything. Robert was terrified of the sasquatch and for good reason. This time, Harriet needed Robert. She had to keep Susan away.

She put the bun behind her back, but Susan stubbornly melted out of the forest. The sasquatch took a step into the clearing and looked from Harriet to the cabin.

"Go away, Susan. I don't want you here. I need to be on my own."

The words made Harriet's throat tighten. She loved her sasquatch friend, but this was not the time to be with her. Harriet told herself she was lying because she didn't have the language to explain what was going on. Susan took a step closer to Harriet. The sasquatch tilted her head and waited. Harriet didn't have time for her forest friend. There wasn't even a moment for a hug. Harriet didn't want shelter. She didn't need company. She wanted to catch a spy before medical secrets got to the enemy.

A twig snapped. Susan looked into the trees and sniffed the air. Harriet had to protect Robert and get rid of Susan. "You've got to go. This is my battle, part of our human war. I have to deal with someone evil."

Susan took a step towards the trap. Harriet clenched her fists and swallowed a scream. Her sasquatch friend refused to listen. She threw the bun as hard as she could. It hit Susan in the chest, fell to the ground and rolled towards the hidden rope.

Susan bounded after the treat. The animal's hands reached out and grabbed it. In the blink of an eye, the sapling shot upright, the rope went taut and Susan was left dangling six feet in the air, with a rope around her hairy wrists. The flash bulb exploded with light. Susan released a howl so loud and long that Harriet shook with terror.

"Susan, Susan, calm down," Harriet said. Panic made it hard to think. "Why didn't you listen to me? Stay still. I can get you down."

Harriet tried to untie the knot on the sapling but Susan's weight, the rain and Harriet's shaking fingers made it impossible to loosen the hold. Susan now occupied the trap set for the doctor. The animal who was to protect her from the orderlies was dangling above the ground, and the only photos being taken were of a sasquatch.

"Robert, save some film for the doctor."

Susan lifted her feet to the rope and pulled herself up until her teeth bit into the knot binding her wrists together. Feet, teeth, hands and body all worked against the trap while Harriet tried to release the rope from below. Suddenly, Susan stopped. Her nostrils flared. Harriet followed Susan's eyes and saw Robert appear from the trees.

"We need to get that thing out of here." Robert's voice came into the clearing. Anger burned into Harriet's scalp.

Harriet turned on her cousin and screamed, "Get back in position. Stay out of sight. Leave Susan to me."

Robert grabbed Harriet's arm and tried to pull her away. "That thing will kill us both. We have to get out of here."

Susan's eyes drilled into Robert. She bared her teeth and growled. Then released a second roar. Robert turned and ran for the cover of the trees. Harriet called after him, "Don't leave. The doctor will be here soon. We need those photos."

Harriet wanted to follow Robert and make sure he stayed to do his job, but she couldn't leave Susan suffering in the trap she'd laid. She hesitated. Her head turned from Susan's body, struggling against the rope, to the forest, quiet and still.

"Robert, are you there?" Silence. "Robert?" Even Harriet could hear the terror in her voice as she calculated the time it would take to reset the trap, get to the camera and gather all the evidence herself.

"I'm still here but, release that thing, and I won't be."

Harriet tried to figure out a fresh plan, but her brain wouldn't work in her tiny, cold, wet and terrified body. Then, the rumble of an engine came along the rocky, wet road. Harriet saw a second camera flash. Like a light bulb being switched on, an alternative scheme sprang into her mind and Harriet stood in the path of headlights. The ambulance came to a halt and the orderlies, followed by the doctor, clambered out of the cab.

"Well, well, well," the doctor said. "What do we have here?"

# CHAPTER TWENTY-THREE
## POLICE

The doctor placed a hand on Harriet's injured shoulder and shoved her towards the orderlies. Then he removed a needle from his case and walked to Susan's writhing body.

"Don't hurt her," Harriet cried. "This is the creature that made the medicine in the forest."

"Did she? Interesting? Let's all go inside and talk for a while."

The doctor stabbed the needle into Susan's leg, waited for the beast to hang limply from the rope, and placed an arm around Harriet's shoulders. Harriet stared at her friend and looked for any sign of life.

The doctor barked orders at the men, "Bring the beast and the patient inside. You, my dear, are going to tell us about the medicines."

Harriet's heart broke inside her chest. She'd betrayed her friend to the one person she knew would misuse the information. She watched helplessly as the orderlies released the rope and carried Susan into the cabin. Her only hope lay with Robert. She listened carefully. Rain fell and feet squelched as they carried her mother into the cabin. Then, from the forest, Harriet heard the unmistakable click of a camera shutter. Harriet coughed loudly to cover the noise and moved into the cabin with Dr. Smith.

Once inside, the doctor tore some paper from his notebook and scribbled a note. He turned to the orderlies and said, "Deliver this. We're moving out tonight, just as soon as this young lady tells me about the miracle cure."

Harriet listened to the ambulance driving away. She only hoped that Robert had taken enough photos and could get evidence to the police before it was too late. She had to kill time.

"If I can get my herbs, I'll show you everything I know," Harriet said.

"Do you think I was born yesterday? You're not leaving here until I know the secrets," the doctor replied. "Guard these two with your lives. I'll fetch your precious herb tin."

Dr. Smith ran out into the rain. Harriet raced to her mother, then to her bound friend. She placed her hand near each of their mouths and sighed with relief as she felt their breath entering and leaving their bodies. By the time the doctor returned with her herb collection, Harriet knew exactly how to delay the doctor's departure.

Harriet asked for some light for her work. After a few minutes, the inside of the cabin buzzed with the sound of a kerosene lamp. Dark shadows danced on the walls as Harriet reached for the mortar and pestle. She ground the herbs slowly and deliberately while the doctor sat at the tiny table with his notebook and pen.

Inside, Harriet prayed Robert had reached the police station while her body went through the motion of making her mom's medicine. She cut the leaves, roots and stems of plants, then carefully mixed them together. The doctor drew the plants and wrote everything he saw.

"What did you use to make this into the paste I found?" the doctor asked.

Harriet's eyes drifted from the bowl to her mother and then the sasquatch. Both were in a deep sleep. The rattle in her mom's breathing had returned. Harriet had to get proper medicine to her, and fast. Her mom wouldn't remember this, but what of her friend. Harriet had been told animals have no souls, but she knew differently. Susan had a family and feelings. She knew love and loss. Surely Susan would understand. Harriet had to do something. She couldn't bear the thought of her mom dying.

Harriet needed Susan's saliva as the missing ingredient, the element that shifted the healing herbs to become a miracle cure. She could take it now and save her mother. Harriet justified her actions to herself. The information so freely given to her would capture a criminal. That had to be a good thing.

The doctor stood and walked to the camp bed. He held Harriet's mom's wrist in his hand and twisted his watch towards the dancing light. Then he took a stethoscope from his bag and listened to his patient's chest.

"Her breathing is getting worse again and her pulse is racing," the doctor said.

"This'll be ready soon."

Getting the medicine to her mother became the most important thing on Harriet's mind. She picked up the bowl, walked to her sleeping friend, collected spittle on the pestle and mixed it into the plant mash. If they were alone in the forest, she'd have laughed and wiped the spit from her friend's face. The doctor's eyes bore into her. His voice made her jump.

"Spit! That's disgusting! The germs could kill your mother."

Harriet nodded her head. She was saving her mother, betraying a friend and helping the enemy all at the same time. Who was she? Where was Robert? The doctor knew the secret ingredient. There was no reason for him to stay. He could leave at any moment. All Harriet could do was to give the mixture to her mother and hope the police arrived in time.

Harriet rolled some mash into a small ball and walked to her mom. She gave her mom a kiss on the forehead and placed the medicine inside her mouth. The doctor held his patient's wrist and waited. A smile covered his face. He took his stethoscope and listened. Harriet could see the blanket rise and fall at a slower pace. Surely, her mom's life was more important than a friendship with an animal. But Harriet didn't believe her own words. Susan had risked everything and found Harriet the help she needed. Guilt swam through Harriet's mind. Her friend was lying unconscious on the floor and Harriet had used her, taken the saliva to heal her mom. Harriet tried to turn her thoughts against Susan. It was easier if she was another enemy. Susan had been in the forest alone. Perhaps she deserved the slap across the face. Maybe she'd been thrown out for a reason. She could have betrayed her family just like the doctor was betraying his country. Stray animals existed. Maybe Susan was a stray for a reason —exiled, rejected and Harriet had looked after her. She'd taken a bullet for Susan. The sasquatch owed her. A life for a life.

Susan snorted and flung her head. Harriet jumped. She stared at her friend, willing the animal to stay asleep. Her mother lay motionless. Harriet left the camp bed and walked to the area where Susan lay bound on the floor. She'd tried to hate her friend but couldn't. All Harriet felt was gratitude and guilt. She sat on the floor beside her friend and stroked her protruding eyebrow. The animal grunted and settled. Harriet listened as the rain tumbled onto the roof.

"Hurry," she said to herself. "Robert, you have to get here soon."

Then, in the distance, came the sound of an engine. Harriet's heart started beating faster. She wanted to know if it was the police car or the orderlies returning to help the doctor.

Dr. Smith tossed Harriet a blanket.

"Cover that thing and keep your little mouth shut," the doctor said.

Harriet stood and saw headlights shining back at her. She dropped the blanket on Susan, leaving the sasquatch's face and legs exposed. Then Harriet raced for the door and ran out into the wet night. Muddy water sloshed over her shoes as she jumped from the patio. She blinked her eyes and forced them to adjust to the night. A car door swung open and out stepped the police officer she'd been waiting for.

"Quick," Harriet called. "He's in here. He drugged my mom and is running his experiments on her."

Harriet ran back up the steps and swung open the cabin door. She stood in the doorway and shouted, "You're under arrest."

The police officer was two steps behind Harriet. His heavy footsteps stopped in the doorway. Harriet turned to see the officer shaking his head in disbelief.

"What do we have here?" the officer asked. "You didn't tell me about this, brother."

"Brother!" Harriet yelled.

The two men laughed.

"Loughlin Mills is a small town," the doctor said. "Harriet, let me introduce you to our new police chief, my brother, Officer Smith."

Harriet's stomach sunk to the floor. All her planning had been for nothing.

"We look after each other," Officer Smith said. "But Dr. Smith, you've been careless."

The officer held out Robert's camera. "Let's see what we have here?"

Harriet tried to reach forward and grab the evidence from the doctor's hand, but he pushed her away. Harriet fell to the ground. She sat up and watched Officer Smith open the back of the camera, hold the film in his fingers and pull. Harriet knew exposure to the light would ruin the pictures Robert had taken.

"What a shame!" Officer Smith said. "A photo of this creature could earn me a fortune."

He turned to his brother and added, "You didn't tell me about capturing Big Foot. I'm impressed. When you told me we would earn a fortune from your discoveries, I thought you were talking about your crazy cures. I didn't think for a moment we could actually earn a fortune. What's the plan? Sell it to a zoo or use it for medical research, then stuff it for a museum?"

"No. You can't. You can't hurt her," Harriet cried. "I won't let you. Robert won't let you. Auntie Helen won't let you."

She crawled across the cabin floor to Susan and threw her arms around the animal's body. Officer Smith walked to Harriet. He grabbed some rope from a hook hanging from a wooden beam, tied her hands and feet together, and left her on the floor.

"You won't get away with this," Harriet said.

"Gag her," Dr.Smith said. "I can't think with all this racket going on."

Officer Smith took a handkerchief from his pocket, forced it between Harriet's teeth and tied it roughly behind her head. The material cut into the corners of her mouth.

"Your cousin thinks he's done his part. I sent him home to bed," Officer Smith said. "As for your aunt, she's tired too. Your little jaunts into the forest have exhausted everyone, they're yesterday's news. Weren't you told the story of *The Boy Who Cried Wolf?* My guess is she'll go to the bakery as usual and see if her little runaway is back when she gets hungry."

Harriet closed her eyes and opened them again. She willed herself to wake up and find out this was a nightmare. She felt her wet clothes on her skin. Rain fell on the cabin roof. She thought of Robert and Annie both wrapped up in bed, confident they had played their part in tonight's plan. Officer Smith was right. No one would come for her. She was alone.

Harriet looked around the cabin. The two men whispered, Harriet's mom slept on the camp bed, and Susan lay on the floor —tied up and helpless. Harriet wormed her way across the floor until she felt her wet skin touch Susan's fur. She curled her body against the curve of Susan's back. If only she could turn back time and think of a better plan. The doctor already knew the secret ingredient. Now, the person who came to the rescue, the officer who was meant to arrest the doctor and declare Harriet a hero, was, in fact, related. A brother. Smith. How stupid could one twelve-year-old be?

The doctor loaded herb jars into a box.

"We don't have time for that," Officer Smith said. "It won't be long before this girl is missed, and that pesky boy knows exactly where we are."

A smile crept over Harriet's face. Robert even annoyed this criminal. It was his way, but this time she was proud of her cousin.

"You should have brought him with you," the doctor said.

"Kidnap doesn't come as easily to me," his brother replied. "Come on. We have to get out of here."

"I'm not leaving without these."

The two men stood looking at each other for a few seconds. Harriet held her breath. The doctor broke the stalemate and resumed his packing. The officer picked up a full box and walked out of the cabin. Harriet listened to the footsteps as they sloshed through puddles. The trunk opened, then footsteps returned. Harriet had to do something. She'd led the doctor to the medicine. She'd help get Germans back into battle. Her father, uncle and Annie's dad would all fight the enemy. Dr. Smith would heal them and send them back to kill again. This war would go on forever. She wished her fury matched Susan's. Harriet felt small and helpless. A child against an evil doctor and police officer did not stand a chance.

Unless…she channelled Susan's anger. Harriet wondered if Susan had been in control when she attacked Robert. The sasquatch may take her anger out on any human in her path. Susan twitched. It was only a matter of time before she released animal fury. Harriet had to focus Susan's anger on the doctor.

Susan's body shuddered. The sedation was wearing off. Harriet looked up. The two men were busy loading boxes into the police car. Harriet hunched her shoulders, dropped her hands below her backside and wriggled her legs through the loop between her arms. She moved her body like a worm until her hands were next to the rope that bound Susan's legs. In the shadows, Harriet worked at the knot until it loosened and fell to the floor. Next, Harriet released Susan's hands. A growl came from Susan's lips. Harriet had to wake her friend. If Susan attacked her, it was nothing worse than she deserved.

Harriet inched her body away from Susan. She knew she couldn't hide from the sasquatch. If Susan woke up and saw the doctor and his brother first, Harriet hoped they would get the force of her rage.

Harriet felt wind hit her as the cabin door opened.

"Come on," Officer Smith said. "We have to get away from here."

"Stop panicking and take this," the doctor said.

He handed his brother a box, and the officer walked back to the door. The movement had not woken Susan. Harriet dragged herself back across the floor. The dry dirt scraped Harriet's skin and her shoulder throbbed with pain. Harriet gritted her teeth. This was nothing compared with the beating of her heart and the thought that ripped through her stomach. She had betrayed her friend.

The door swung open again.

"I'm leaving," Officer Smith said. "You can come with me or get yourself out of this mess."

Harriet looked at the men. The doctor removed a syringe from his bag and drew liquid into it.

"I said I'm leaving!"

"Not without that," the doctor said.

They both looked at Susan. Harriet held her breath, closed her eyes and prayed Susan would wake up.

# CHAPTER TWENTY-FOUR
## THE BATTLE

"Are you serious?" Officer Smith asked. "That thing weighs a ton. How are we going to get it into the car? Have you seen the size of that creature?"

"That creature holds the secret I've been searching for. Something in it's saliva has cured tuberculosis. This is huge. World shattering. If I can identify the chemical responsible and reproduce it in a lab, I'll go down in medical history with Alexander Fleming and Madame Curie."

As the two men argued, Harriet inched her body towards Susan's head. She held the enormous skull in her bound hands and tried to turn Susan's head to face her. Susan's nostrils flared and, as if by instinct, she bared her teeth. Their eyes met. Susan frowned. Harriet knew the power Susan possessed, and shuddered.

Harriet lifted her bound hands to Susan's face. She stroked Susan's protruding eyebrow ridge. The sasquatch pushed her away. Harriet crawled back. She had to wake Susan up, provoke a reaction. Harriet touched Susan's lips. Susan shook her head. Her eyes opened and closed as she tried to focus on the surrounding room.

"She's waking up," the doctor said.

He walked towards the sasquatch, syringe in hand. Harriet threw her body over Susan's.

"No! I won't let you!" Harriet screamed.

"Get her off this animal!" the doctor shouted.

Officer Smith picked Harriet up. Her shoulder burned with a pain Harriet knew she deserved. She kicked her legs and screamed. The doctor took the last two paces to the sasquatch and raised the syringe high into the air, ready to plunge the needle deep into Susan's side.

"No!" Harriet cried. "Don't hurt her! You can't hurt her!"

At the sound of Harriet's cry, Susan's eyes opened. She jumped up, swayed unsteadily on her legs, grabbed the doctor and tossed him against the wall. The glass syringe flew out of his hand and shattered into a hundred pieces.

Susan's eyes fixed on Officer Smith. Her nostrils flared and her body hunched. In slow motion, the police officer placed Harriet down and stepped to the door. Susan let out a roar. Officer Smith turned and ran out into the rain. He hurled himself from the porch, landed in a muddy puddle, slipped and fell. Susan charged after him. The drugs had slowed her movements, but Harriet watched in awe at the power in the sasquatch's body. Officer Smith scrambled through the mud, desperate to get away from this wild animal. Susan stood over him in a heartbeat. She picked up the officer, held him high over her head and threw him against a tree. Man versus beast in hand-to-hand combat. No sooner had Officer Smith stirred than Susan was there, breathing hard and salivating over her enemy. The sasquatch picked up Officer Smith and tossed him against the car. There was a loud thud, followed by a splash in an enormous puddle.

Bang! Harriet turned to see the doctor aiming a rifle at Susan. The sasquatch let out a cry. She clutched her arm and turned to the doctor. The rifle was reloaded in seconds.

"No! No, you can't kill her! She's my friend," Harriet yelled.

"Friend? You showed me the miracle in her saliva. You used her," the doctor said.

"Stop! Stop!" Harriet cried.

The doctor turned the gun on Harriet.

"I've had enough of you," Dr. Smith said.

He took a step towards Harriet and aimed the rifle at her. She curled herself into a ball, covered her head, and waited.

Then from out of the darkness the earth seemed to shake. A battle cry erupted that stunned everyone and made them all turn to face the trees. Sasquatches of every shape and size followed the noise. Harriet recognized the huge warrior leading the charge— the sasquatch who had struck Susan.

Officer Smith scrambled from his muddy resting place, opened the car door and slid inside. A small sasquatch turned as the car door closed and jumped on the hood. Others followed. Soon, sasquatches covered the car. They climbed, leaped and screamed at the man inside. Harriet remembered the story about the hunter being torn apart and wondered if that fate would fall on Officer Smith.

She hid behind some boxes on the patio, terrified by the fury she'd unleashed. A mechanical click took her attention from the barking apes to the doctor. The mob on the car froze. Quickly, the doctor cocked his rifle and fired. The smallest sasquatch flew through the air and landed in a heap on the ground. The rest of the troop looked in stunned silence at their fallen comrade. They growled in unison, a low rumble that made Harriet's hairs stand on end. Together they moved off the car towards the doctor. They surrounded the doctor, picked him up and lifted him above their heads.

Behind them, the car engine started up, and headlights cast enormous shadows across the clearing. Wheels spun as the car sped up, bounced across the clearing and drove straight at the attacking animals. Some jumped out of the way, but it bowled over those in the centre. One bounced over the car roof and fell on the ground. Others were knocked to the side like ten pins at the bowling alley as they dropped the doctor. Officer Smith leaned over and opened the passenger door. The doctor scrambled towards freedom, but the biggest sasquatch grabbed him by the ankle and swung him above his head like a lasso. When the limp rag of a man was released, his body hit the car with a deafening clunk. The sasquatch hit his fists against his chest and grunted rhythmically. His troop joined him until they were all stamping and shouting together. They banded together and moved in for the attack.

The doctor scrambled over the hood and crawled through the open car door. With legs still struggling to get into the car, Officer Smith slammed the car into reverse, then slammed on the brakes, turned one hundred and eighty degrees, changed gears and sped down the logging road. The sasquatch leader followed, barking orders to his warriors who ran or limped behind him.

Harriet watched and waited for their noise to fade into the distance. Her body shook, her shoulder ached, and her heart felt as if it would jump out of her chest. She glanced in through the cabin window. Her mother lay on the camp bed looking peaceful and serene. Rain beat down on the porch roof and ran trickling from the gutter. Slowly, Harriet looked around. Sasquatches lay in the mud, some clutched injured arms and legs, others were motionless. Harriet came out of her hiding place and wandered around the battlefield until she found Susan, still and silent.

Harriet threw herself on the giant wet rag. "Susan. Don't die. Please, don't die. I'm sorry, so sorry. This is my fault, all my fault. I wanted to catch the doctor. Now, he's got away and I've killed you."

Tears and rain fell down Harriet's cheeks. She heard them splashing into the tire tracks and footprints, washing away the evidence of the battle. She moved close to Susan's still face, traced her fingers over her ridged eyebrows and across her flat nose. Was this what war was about? Intense fighting followed by pain, emptiness and a heart that would never heal. The doctor had fired the shot but, if Susan died, Harriet knew she'd killed the only loyal friend she had. She leaned in and touched her lips to her friend's hollow cheek.

Harriet replayed the night's events in her mind. She'd made Annie pretend she was sick, even though she didn't want to lie. She'd sent Robert to fetch the police, only to find he was an enemy. She'd trapped her friend by mistake, then shown the doctor the miracles of the forest, hoping it would buy enough time for an arrest. Now, the doctor and police officer had shot Susan, got away and injured Susan's family. No one would ever trust her again. Harriet sat back and wished she could start over.

"Live. Please, live. I got everything wrong."

Harriet stopped, jumped up and ran into the cabin. She raced back to Susan carrying a tiny ball of the medicine from her mother's mouth. She knelt in the mud and placed the ball inside Susan's lips.

A tear rolled down her face and dripped onto Susan's eyelid. It fluttered.

"Susan. Can you hear me? Are you alive?"

The giant creature's eye opened, and the corner of her mouth twitched into a half smile.

"Susan!" Harriet yelled.

Harriet threw herself onto Susan and hugged her friend. Then, a feeling of being watched, made her look up. Harriet's eyes darted to the trees. Something was there. She stood and walked to the cabin. Slowly, she opened the door, hid inside and looked out the window.

Out of the forest came the band of sasquatches. Some limped, others supported an arm or held their ribs. They surrounded Susan and the other sasquatches, lifted limp bodies from the ground, supported fallen comrades and retreated.

Harriet wanted to call out, tell them she was sorry, but words wouldn't come. The sasquatch family came back. They'd returned for their own, and they left Harriet alone with her sick mother.

"Harriet?"

The sound of her name startled her. It was like a quiet whisper in the trees, barely audible above the rain.

"Harriet?"

There it was again. Harriet knew the voice, and her heart wanted to burst open with relief. She turned, ran across the cabin and hugged her mother.

"Harriet, where are we? And what's going on?"

"Mom, you're awake."

"And feeling a little better. But where are we?"

The sound of tires, splashing through the mud, made Harriet jump.

"Stay still, Mom. Pretend you're asleep."

Harriet hid in the corner and listened. Her eyes fell on the box of saliva balls. Maybe the doctor had returned for the precious medicine. She picked up the box, held it to her chest and waited.

Footsteps echoed across the porch. The door burst open. There stood Robert, Annie, Auntie Helen, Mrs. McLoughlin, and behind them Herr Schmidt.

Harriet threw herself into Annie's open arms. The box pressed into her skin, full of medicine to heal her mother. No one would separate her from the treasured contents.

Harriet broke away from the embrace and stood on the exposed film on the cabin floor. Robert's eyes followed his cousin's movements.

"Where's my camera?" Robert asked. "Officer Smith took it as evidence."

"Evidence?" Herr Schmidt asked.

Robert picked up the kerosene lamp and searched the wreck of the cabin. He found the Box Brownie and picked it up. The back flapped open like a broken Jack-in-the-box, and there was a crack across the lens.

"You owe me a new camera," Robert said.

"It wasn't my fault," Harriet said.

"Whose fault was it?" Robert asked.

Harriet looked at Herr Schmidt. She wanted to reply, to tell her cousin they had stopped evil experiments in the forest, but she stopped herself. Herr Schmidt was standing right there, listening. He could still be involved. No one had proved he wasn't a German spy working for the Fuhrer. The horrors of the night washed over her. Susan had been shot, her wild tribe had carried her away, and a suspected enemy agent stood in front of her. Harriet sunk to the floor and cried.

"Cry baby bunting," Robert sung.

"Robert, enough," Auntie Helen shouted. "You, young lady, need to get into dry clothes. And this is no place for someone with bad lungs. You can tell us how you got here and what you've been doing when we get home."

Herr Schmidt walked to the bed and lifted Harriet's mom into his arms. It was time to go home.

# CHAPTER TWENTY-FIVE
## TRUTH

Harriet sat at the kitchen table, knowing her mother was safely asleep. Day was breaking and the warmth from the stove filled the room. Annie sat on one side of her and Robert on the other. Auntie Helen and Mrs. McLoughlin sat in stunned silence as they listened to the events of the night. Herr Schmidt had left them to fetch the police. Harriet had tried to explain that Officer Smith left with his brother, but Herr Schmidt didn't seem to believe her.

"We had to keep the doctor in town so Harriet could set the trap," Annie said. "Sorry Mom, I wasn't really sick."

"This is unbelievable," Auntie Helen said.

"It's all true," Harriet said.

"I saw the ambulance arrive," Robert said. "I took photos."

"But the doctor," Mrs. McLoughlin said.

The telephone rang and made everyone jump. Auntie Helen got up, walked to the hallway and answered it. From the kitchen they could hear her say "Oh", "Really", "Hmm, I see", and "Yes" repeatedly.

"That was Herr Schmidt," Auntie Helen explained. "He says there's no sign of Officer or Dr. Smith."

"I told you, they've left," Harriet said.

"Maybe you should write this down. *The Three Mills Gazette* should hear a story like this," Auntie Helen said.

"Yes!" Harriet shouted. "Breaking news! Local trio expose evil experiments in the forest."

Harriet ran from the kitchen to get her notebook and pencil.

It wasn't long before Harriet, Annie and Robert jumped on bikes and cycled to Brennan. They picked up the photos from the pharmacy, stopped by the newspaper office and delivered Harriet's story to Mr. Gunner.

"Stop the press!" Harriet announced.

The news editor smiled, sat up and took the envelope from Harriet.

"And what might this be?"

"Remember me? Harriet Hall, a journalist from London, England currently living in Loughlin. This is the scoop of the century."

"Is it indeed?" Mr. Gunner asked. "Leave it with me."

He handed Harriet, Robert and Annie three coins and said, "Why don't you buy some candy. I'll have a look at this and see what you have."

"You won't be disappointed, but publish the story soon or I'll take it to another paper. *The Times* are next on my list."

"I'll read it straight away, Harriet Hall of London, England, now living in Loughlin. If it's as good as you say, your name will be in print with the next edition of *The Gazette*."

On Saturday, Harriet raced to Herr Schmidt's shop as soon as she'd finished her weekend chores and given her mother another dose of medicine. She grabbed *The Three Mills Gazette* from its stand at the front of the shop and stared at the front page.

"Local Doctor and Police Chief Lead the Way. The Smith brothers of Loughlin, B.C. have volunteered to fight tyranny. They've joined the growing number of our brave citizens who have joined up. Their courage and skills will be missed, but we at

*The Three Mills Gazette* wish them, and all the men and women fighting abroad, a speedy victory and a safe return."

Harriet could not believe the words written in black and white. She stormed into the store, fuming about the lies printed in the paper. Harriet wanted to scream and shout, but swallowed her words when she saw Herr Schmidt standing behind the counter. He smiled at Harriet and she forced a smile in return.

"Just the paper?" he asked.

Harriet nodded and took the money from her pocket. The familiar poster behind the counter caught her eye. "Careless talk costs lives." Harriet bit the inside of her cheek, handed over her money and ran to the bakery. She slammed the paper onto Robert's flour-covered overalls.

"Have you seen this? It's outrageous! I'm going to give that news editor a piece of my mind."

Robert read the front page and handed the paper back to Harriet. "I told you, adults don't listen to kids."

Harriet opened her mouth to argue, but Robert said, "I'm nearly done here, and the shop closes in a few minutes. Help me clear up, then we'll get Annie and go to Brennan. *Swiss Family Robinson* is on at the movies."


Harriet spoke non-stop as Robert cycled and she bounced around in the breadbasket. Her anger grew with each sentence uttered. She needed to know how Mr. Gunner could print such lies. She'd uncovered a conspiracy, but here were the Smith brothers being hailed as heroes. Harriet jumped to the ground outside the newspaper offices and ran into the building. Annie and Robert were a few steps behind.

"What's this?" Harriet shouted.

She threw the paper onto the editor's desk.

"Well, good afternoon, Miss Hall. I didn't expect to see you so soon."

"Where's my story?"

"Ah, yes. You write well, Miss Hall. It was a wonderful story."

"So why didn't you print it?"

"Evidence."

"We gave you the photos."

"Grainy pictures of herb jars on a shelf do not make up evidence. You accused a doctor and a police officer of working for Hitler and conducting illegal experiments."

"They were."

"But I can't print stories like that without a lot of evidence. As for your mythical sasquatch…"

"They're real, as real as you and I."

Mr. Gunner leaned back in his chair and placed his feet on his desk. "So you say."

"I'm telling the truth."

"Truth is an interesting idea in the middle of a war. People say they want to read the truth but really, they want to hear their brothers, cousins, fathers and uncles are coming home soon. Do you think they like seeing names of dead soldiers listed on the front page? Or news suggesting the enemy has invaded their hometown?"

"What about my mother's recovery?"

"Now, that is good news. You could write about a miracle, here in The Three Mills. Maybe you could interview a minister to get his views."

Harriet rolled her eyes. "But the cure came from the forest."

"Miss Hall, you have all the makings of a talented journalist. Take this as an advance for your first story that goes to print."

The newspaper editor took a handful of loose change from his pocket and handed it to Harriet.

"Go to the movie theatre. Buy an ice cream. Treat yourself. On your way home, drop in and we can discuss some ideas for your next story. London Evacuee Attends Local School. Kids Collect Scrap Metal for the War Effort. The Three Mills Spelling Bee."

"But…"

"Run along. I have a paper to write."

Robert and Annie pulled Harriet out of the office. She looked at her cousin and new friend. Life seemed unfair, but the warm Saturday afternoon sunshine made it hard for Harriet to stay angry. She'd chased the doctor and police officer away. They might not have been caught, but they couldn't do any more of their experiments in this town. She'd kept everyone safe, and one day she knew everyone would discover the miracle cures in the forest of her new home.

A few weeks later, Auntie Helen prepared a feast to take to the lake.

"The last summer picnic has to be the best," she said. "It's back to school tomorrow."

There was a loud groan from the children. Harriet held her mother's thin arm as she ambled to the water's edge. Each day Harriet's mom could walk a little further. Today, mother and daughter were determined. There was no longer the rattling noise in her lungs. It was only a matter of time before strength returned to her body.

The medicine was almost gone, but it wasn't that that bothered Harriet. Every time she'd given her mother an herb ball, she thought of her friend, the gentle giant in the forest. She hoped Susan was still alive, that she'd recovered from the gunshot. In her heart Harriet knew she'd used her friend. She wanted to catch Herr Schmidt and the doctor—to expose an evil plot to help the Germans. Instead, after the doctor had escaped, Herr Schmidt carried on as if nothing had happened.

Harriet had visited the forest every day. There was no sign of Susan—no smell, no friendly smile, no comforting hugs. She tried to put her betrayal out of her mind, but the howl released when Susan got caught in the trap was the last thing Harriet thought of as she fell asleep and the first thing when she woke up. Even the medicine was bittersweet. It was making her mother better, but Harriet had destroyed a friendship to get it.

Instead of feeling brave and heroic, she felt small and broken. Robert, Billy and Mickey ran to the lake. They played and splashed Annie and her siblings. Her mother and Auntie Helen chatted and laughed with each other on the tartan picnic blanket. Harriet was alone again. She reached for a piece of pie and wandered into the forest. This time she knew she deserved her loneliness. It was the cost of betrayal.

Harriet found the clearing where she'd first met Susan and sat on a rock. She tore a piece of pastry from the pie, threw it to the ground and watched a squirrel pick it up in her paws.

"Go on, take it. It'll fatten you up for winter."

The squirrel shovelled it into its mouth and ran up the fir tree bark.

Harriet smiled as tears rolled down her cheeks.

"Susan, if only I could say sorry. I have so much to thank you for. I don't deserve another chance, but please let me say sorry."

A grunt came from the trees. Harriet froze.

"Susan, is that you?"

Harriet sniffed the air. The smell of wet dog, cooked cabbage and the forest floor wafted into Harriet's nose. She wanted to run around and shout for joy. Instead, she laid the piece of pie on the rock.

"I'm sorry," Harriet said. "You're the best friend I've ever had. I hope one day you'll forgive me. I don't deserve your friendship, but I hope I can be as good a friend to you as you have been to me."

Harriet walked out of the clearing. She heard a rustle of leaves behind her and glanced over her shoulder. Susan's hand lifted the pie to her mouth. Saliva drooled from her smiling lips. The two stared at each other. Harriet's heart thumped in her chest as she took a step towards her friend. The sasquatch's lips curled, showing her huge incisors. A deep growl came from Susan's belly.

Harriet's eyes drifted to the wound on Susan's shoulder. The gunshot was healing well. Slowly, Harriet pulled her blouse from her shoulder, touched her scar and looked at Susan's furless, red raw wound.

"I'm sorry."

Susan's face relaxed into a smile. She placed the pie on the ground, pulled herself to her full height, took two steps across the clearing and threw her huge hairy arms around Harriet. Harriet relaxed into the embrace.

"I will never tell another lie," Harriet said. "From now everything I say and write will be the truth."

Susan relaxed her grip, looked at Harriet and smiled. She wiped a tear from Harriet's cheek, lifted the pie to her mouth, smiled and wandered into the forest. Harriet turned and walked to the lake. There was her mother, Auntie Helen, Robert, Mickey, Billy, Annie and all Annie's siblings.

Harriet's dad was right, adventures were everywhere in this new home. Harriet ran to the picnic blanket, took off her shoes, socks, blouse and shorts to reveal her swimmers. She kissed her mom on the cheek and ran into the water.

"Watch out!" she shouted. "Incoming cluster bomb. Three, two, one, Geronimo!"

Harriet landed with a splash. The lake became a churning mass of children as they splashed, squealed and laughed. It was hard to believe a war was on. Occasionally. Harriet's brain drifted to the dads who would come home as heroes, but while they were waiting, Harriet would be the voice of truth. She'd write for *The Three Mills Gazette*, go to school and live in this town knowing her friends, both human and non-human, were close to her.

Harriet lay in bed that night with a smile on her face. She thought of Susan on her moss bed in the forest, and heard Robert, Billy and Mickey breathing quietly in their sleep. She knew her mother and Auntie Helen were both resting safely. She wondered where her dad was. An image of him commanding sailors on the high sea came to Harriet's mind. She pictured the bombs firing from the ship's cannons, sinking German battle-ships. Victory would come to the allies, but not before Harriet Hall became an international war correspondent. She planned to expose the ugly truth of this war and the enemy hiding in Loughlin. For now, she needed to sleep.

Thank you for reading *Harriet Hall and the Miracle Cure*. If you enjoyed it, please take a moment to leave a review on Amazon, Goodreads, or your preferred online retailer.

Reviews are the best way to show your support for an author and to help new readers discover their books.

## ABOUT THE AUTHOR

Like her heroine, Harriet Hall, Sonia Garrett is no stranger to moving around the world. She was born in England, moved to California when she was three weeks old, went to school in Australia, and spent most of her adult life in England where she graduated from the University of East Anglia with a BA (Hons) in Drama and English. She is always up for an adventure and has worked as a dancer, clown, actor, and business owner. Now, she lives in beautiful British Columbia, Canada and is a mom, teacher, storyteller and writer.

Sonia lives in the gentle chaos of books, outdoor paraphernalia, and cooking ingredients with her daughter, Jacquie, and their French Bulldog, Toast. She loves skiing, hiking, live theatre, and relaxed meals with friends.

For more information visit:
www.soniagarrett.ca

## OTHER TITLES BY SONIA GARRETT:

*Maddie Makes a Movie*
*Maddie Makes Money*

Made in the USA
Middletown, DE
29 October 2021